Navigating Uncertainty

TY WILLIAMS

TAILOR PUBLISHING GROUP

CONTENTS

Author's Note

Hi I'm Ty Williams! I am so glad you have decided to pick up Navigating Uncertainty. Though before you start, let's have a quick talk about some of its content.

Now don't worry, nothing crazy. I want to just make sure you don't read something against your personal preference.

Though this book is a romance between our main couple Jake and Hannah. It is heavily christian and intertwined into the storyline is a LGBTQ character with a very unloving father, a set of orphan twins, a dead sibling, and possibly more. If any of this may trigger you or goes against personal convictions/preferences, please read this book with caution.

YOUR MENTAL & SPIRITUAL HEALTH MATTER!!!

CHAPTER 1

Jake

We had been driving for a couple of hours to reach our new home in Edmond, North Carolina. A young couple freshly engaged, on our way to answer the burning call to the ministry, just a few short months after graduating college.

I look over at my fiancé, " You know, you're really cute when you get frustrated about getting something done like you want it."

She pushed a button on our gps, "Can you help me fix the gps? It stopped working again."

"It's fine, we're almost there anyway; it's the next exit," I say, then go back to focusing on the road. I heard a small sigh escape from my fiancé's lips, "Hannah, what's wrong? Miss family already?"

"No, it's not that," she replied.

"Then what's bothering you, gumdrop?"

She let out another sigh, and put her head in her hands. "I thought about how we're planning a wedding my dad refuses to attend. I really wanted him to walk me down the aisle."

"Yeah, He really doesn't like me for some reason."

"Jake, you wrecked his truck during homecoming back in high school!"

"Oh yeah, that was a wild night. Jace knew how to have some fun," I said, the memory flashing through my mind.

"Y'all raced down the street like idiots."

I could do nothing but laugh at Hannah as we recount one of the most memorable nights of our relationship. I looked up to see that we only had a mile till we got to the town' s exit. I pulled over to the side of the highway and reached over towards Hannah.

"I'm sure he would never miss his only daughter's big wedding, no matter his thoughts on the groom. I'll talk to your mother about it."

"No, it'll just make her worry, I don't want to do that to her," I wrap my arms around Hannah in response, and say "How about some ice cream when we get into town? Will that make you feel better?"

Hannah began to slowly smile at the possibility of getting ice cream. "I'll take that as a yes," I chuckled. I settled back into the driver's seat and took the town's exit.

"Google says the nearest ice cream parlor is a place called Nicole's Ice Cream Shop," Hannah beamed with excitement. "How far are we from it?" I asked.

"Not far, it's right on main street," she answered as we passed the *Welcome to Edmond, North Carolina* sign.

"We have finally arrived at our new home," I happily shared. "Hannah, can you call Claire? We were supposed to let her know when we got here." Hannah nodded and began calling her, placing the phone on speaker before setting it on the console.

As I waited, listening for Claire's voice from an answered call, I spotted the ice cream parlor and drove into its parking lot.

"Hi, this is Claire."

"Hey, this is Jake and Hannah Dawson ..." Hannah said.

"Oh, you must be our new pastors! What can I help you with?" she responded cheerily.

"Indeed we are, we were calling to let you know we made it to Edmond." I replied.

"Yes sir, are you close to the church?"

"No, we are getting some ice cream currently, we will be on the way right after."

"Lovely, I'll see you there!"

Hannah smiled as she said, "See you there, Claire!"

We ended the phone call and got out of the car to walk into the parlor. "So, what flavor do you want, gumdrop?" I asked as I grabbed her hand.

"Um, maybe I'll get cookies and cream or mint chocolate chip," she replied. I open the door for Hannah, and we walk into the parlor to order.

Waiting for us was a petite blonde woman with the biggest smile I've ever seen on a southern woman's face.

"Welcome to Nicole's Ice Cream Parlor! What can I get you?" she asked joyfully.

"Hi, we'll take two cones of cookies and cream please," I replied.

We sat in our car outside of Redemption Fellowship finishing our cookies and cream ice cream cones. "That was some good ice cream, I can see myself becoming a regular there," Hannah said, licking it off her hand.

"Yeah, it was really good ice cream. Let's go in, I bet Claire is waiting for us inside," I told her. We got out of the car, and walked up to the front door. I go to open the door, and find it locked.

"Well, that's odd," I said. Hannah pulls out her phone, and texts Claire:

"There we go, just texted her. She's coming," Hannah said proudly, being the problem solver she loves being. I look over at Hannah, proud to call her my helpmeet. By this time, Claire was holding the door open for us to get in.

"Pastor Jake! Pastor Hannah! How are y'all? Was your drive over ok?" She said excitedly. I could tell that she was one of the church's many social butterflies.

"The drive was fine, we're just a little tired from the ride," I replied as we walked into a beautiful church lobby.

"I just have to get the keys to the parsonage from the office," She said walking us out of the lobby. As she led us to the office door, a hooded man was leaning against the wall.

"Hey Kyle, come say hi to our new pastors," She told him.

"Sup losers," He replied.

I reach out my hand to give him a firm handshake, "Hey dude, what's up! Name's Jake." He just stared at me, I retract my hand awkwardly "Um, nice meeting you."

The office was right across from where Kyle was leaning. Claire went in and grabbed the house keys. "Ok, here are your keys to the parsonage and keys to both of your offices," She said, handing both of us a set of keys. "Is there anything else I can help you with?"

"Um yes, do you know any wedding venues near town?" I asked.

"You're not married already?" She questioned.

"We're engaged, we are trying to plan it currently."

"Oh, how nice .. you can have it here or The Wedding Barn," she said.

"May I ask what's The Wedding Barn?"

"It's an old farm that one of our members turned into a wedding venue," she replied.

"Ok thanks, can you send me the link for the Barn?" Hannah asked.

"Sure, I will do it as soon as I get home," she replied.

We walked back to the car to head to the house we will soon call home. I looked over to Hannah and squeezed her hand, "I love that

I get to do this with you." I opened the passenger door for her, and planted a quick kiss on her cheek.

I get in the car, and pull out of the parking lot. "Hannah, are you considering having the wedding at The Wedding Barn?" I asked.

"I just thought it was worth a look, and no I'm not saying we won't possibly have it at the church. I know you were going to ask that next" She replied.

I turn left onto the street where the house was supposed to be. "Hannah, whatever you think is best is good for me. If you're not happy, there is no point." I drive into the house's driveway and start grabbing my bookbag and Hannah's purse.

"Hannah, I'm going to sit this on the porch and come get you after I unlock the door," I said while walking up the porch. I look at the bright red door, and turn the key to my first ever home, outside of living with my parents or a college dorm.

I run back to the car, and open Hannah's door. I grab her hand, and lead her up the front stairs. At the top of the stairs I pull her close to me, and kiss her like it's already our wedding day. "Now, my dear future wife, welcome to our new home!

CHAPTER 2

Hannah

I walked down the stairs to the kitchen. As long as I've known him, Jake has never been a morning person, so he won't be up for another half hour. I walked over to the coffeemaker, and got a pot started for Jake's breakfast. Then I got my phone off of its charger on the counter. It's a habit of mine to be on my phone right before bed, so I keep it on the charger downstairs.

I went to the grocery store last night, so the fridge is fully stocked. I grabbed fruit for my smoothie, frozen waffles, and some link turkey sausage.

"Morning gumdrop," I heard as I dropped two waffles into the toaster.

"Morning dear," I replied, putting the link sausage into the pan. Jake walks up to me, and hugs me from behind. I tilt my head back a little, giving him a gentle kiss.

"What's on your schedule today, Jake?" I asked while I handed him his coffee. He takes a sip gratefully, and sits at the island.

"I have a meeting with my new assistant over coffee," he answered. I plated two waffles and a couple of the link sausages, and handed it to him.

"That's exciting! What time is that going to be? I want to go check out the wedding barn." He checked the calendar on his phone. "It's in about half an hour; I can meet you there after."

"Yeah sure, I'll call Claire to take me over there."

"Ok, we also have to start setting up our office," He replied while putting his plate in the sink.

"Yeah, we can do that right after," I replied.

Brring-Brring, I picked up my phone to my very cheerful mother on the other end.

"Hi mom," I answered quickly before she went into her weekly rant about how she can't see me as often as she likes.

"Hi hun, I was calling to see how y'all are settling into the new home," she answered back. I waited to see what else she had to ask. This couldn't be the only reason she called.

"Everything's going well. We have a few errands to take care of today," I answered.

"That's good. I was worried about you not having everything you need."

"We're totally fine. Do you need anything else, mom?" I asked as Jake walked back into the kitchen.

"Is that your mom or mine?" He asked.

"It's my mom, dear," I answered.

"Tell her I said hello, got to go meet my assistant now" I return to the call with my mother

"Hi Jake," she said before I could even relay the message. *"Now, Hannah, did you get the email of wedding venues you can check out next time you visit home?"*

"Mom, we're going to have the wedding here. We're looking at a venue today," I told her

"Oh well, I guess I'll tell your father he has to drive me down." she said, not wanting to deal with my father's stubbornness.

"Yes ma'am, I am going to come back to visit once we've fully settled into our new jobs and the new house."

"Ok, talk to you later. Love you," she said with disappointment.

"Love you, mom," I hung the phone up just in time to feel a smack on the ass. I turn around to find Jake standing at the sink.

"I thought you left to have coffee with your assistant," I asked with confusion. I wrapped my arms around him and held on tight.

"He needed to push it back a couple of hours," he answered. "We got some time to waste, want to cuddle on the couch and watch some tv?"

"Is that even a question? Yes, I do" I answered and ran up stairs to grab a blanket to share with my love.

CHAPTER 3

Jake

I was sitting in a booth at the far back of Saint's Den, the coffee lounge where I asked my assistant to meet me. I looked around the cafe, excited to see that the lounge was just as full as the location over on campus back at college.

They used to let us host a young adults' group there. I started to wonder if this location will allow us to do the same.

"Are you Jake?" I looked up to see a black haired, scrawny teenager, who appeared to be around 17 years old. He wore a black and yellow Nirvana shirt, skinny jeans, and had a few piercings.

"Yes, indeed I am" I stood up and offered my hand. He shook my hand, and sat down on the other side of the booth.

"Ok Jake! My name is Finley, those close to me call me Fin, you are not close to me. If you expect to get some bubbly assistant like Claire, I am not it, I am devoted, but I will be very blunt at times with no remorse. I will do my job and only my job. Any questions?" He sipped his coffee, which I didn't even see in his hand at first.

"Finley, it is nice to meet you. It's good that you are devoted to the job, though I want to learn more about you, more than talk about you being my assistant the whole time," I said to him.

"There is no need, to be honest," he stated. "If you think that we are going to be work buddies, it's not going to happen. Like I said before, I am devoted to my job, and that is what this is. They needed someone to be your assistant, so I applied," he said firmly.

I sat there looking at my assistant with a quick newfound respect for such a young man being able to to stand his ground. "Finley, I respect that, and I think this will be a great partnership going forward."

"Oh is that so, was this so you could get a head start at judging me?" He stood up from the booth. "I will not sit here, and be judged by another so-called pastor."

I looked at him, and could see all the past pain in his eyes. "Finley, that's not what I meant at all. I was just trying to express that after meeting you, I'm very excited to work with you." I got up and offered my hand, "Now, understand that I will never judge you harshly or force you to do anything you're not comfortable with."

Finley wiped his face, and sat back down on his side of the table, "Ok, but can I explain something to you?" I looked confused at the question, but was glad he seemed to open up some.

"Of course, you can, Finley," I answered.

He seemed to relax a little, "I'm not going to be very open around you like you most likely want. I've been hurt by multiple past pastors, this is going to be hard if we're going to move forward."

I sat across the booth from Finley with an aching heart over the pain that many like them had to endure because of the lack of knowledge and maturity that previous pastors had when handling his soul.

"Okay Finley, I'm going let you go for now. I will see you Sunday morning in my office at 9:00 sharp."

He looked at me a little puzzled, "Dude, church doesn't start till 12:00."

"I like to go over my sermon notes prior to service and I also want to observe how the church prepares for service each week." I answered.

He slowly nods at this, and grabs a couple of papers from his crimson black satchel.

"Before I go, here is the paperwork the board told me to give you, just in case you want to redo anything in the office. Now, I have quite a way to walk home. If you need me before then, you have my number," He said, walking over to the cashier.

"Finley, I can give you a ride home, you don't have to walk," I said. He looked over at me, and rolled his eyes, while ordering a new coffee.

"Dude, it's fine! I walk home all the time." he pulled out his wallet to pay for the order. "I know that your past experience wasn't very great. I promise that this will be better. Now, I insist that you allow me, your new pastor, to take you home."

He again rolls his eyes "Fine, where's your car at?" He grabbed his coffee, and followed me outside to the car.

"I'm right over here," I answered as I pushed the button on my key fob.

We got in and I dialed Hannah's number to let her know I was done, and going to take Finley home. *"Hey Jake, Are you finished with the meeting already?"* she answered.

"Yeah, I'm taking Finley home so he doesn't have to walk." I replied.

"Oh lovely, tell him I said hi. Also I called The Wedding Barn and they are currently closed, it will be open on Monday." I could hear the disappointment in her voice, Hannah loved event planning. It took so much effort for her to wait till we got to Edmond to start wedding planning.

"Ok, I'll make sure I save time on Monday to go check it out with you" I assured her,

"What time are y'all going? I'll make sure it's on your schedule" I heard Finley ask.

"Um, I don't have anything around noon, I just have to be done by three to attend the women's Bible study group."

"Okay, that works, Pastor Hannah. It's on his schedule" Finley said firmly. "Oh, also I live on the next street, the first house." He added. I turned onto the street, and parked in front of the house.

"Alright, here you go, Finley. It was good to meet you, man. If you ever need me to pick you up, let me know, I don't like that my new assistant is walking everywhere."

"Whatever dude, I'll see you Sunday morning unless you need something before then," He said as he got out. "Oh, and bye, Pastor Hannah."

"See you Sunday, Finley," She replied back. *"Jake, I don't feel like fixing dinner, you want to go out to eat instead?"*

"We can do that. What do you have a taste for, gumdrop?" I asked.

"Um honestly, I don't know, let me google some local restaurants" she responded. *"There is a June's Soul Food,"*

"If that's what you want, that's where we will go. You know I'm easy to please," I told her. "I'm actually almost home. Finley doesn't live that far from us."

"Ok dear, I'll let you go and get changed out of my hoodie and leggings." She said then hung up the phone.

I let out a big sigh, thinking about the day I first met Hannah at a church lock-in during our sophomore year of high school. I needed a few more volunteer hours before the semester ended to qualify for a summer program I wanted to attend. She was trying for the same program and offered the lock-in at her church. After I saw her that night, I made it my mission to make her mine.

CHAPTER 4

Hannah

As we drive up The Wedding Barn, I smile at how beautiful everything looked so far. I looked at all of the farmland, and how well kept it seemed to be.

"This looks like a perfect place to have the wedding. Lots of room for us to host both families and the church." Jake said, looking over at me as he parked at the far end of the Barn.

"Hey Reverend Dawson and Lady Belle. So good to see y'all today." A petite woman yelled as she came running out of the Barn. "My name is Julie and welcome to The Wedding Barn!" I smiled at how chipper Julie genuinely was. I had a great conversation with her after church yesterday about my sermon where I preached "She Can't Fall with Him."

"Just Hannah is fine, Ms. Julie! Thank you for letting us come check out the venue. I know you're very busy with the great upkeep of this place."

Julie released a big chuckle at this statement, "Hannah, it's no problem. Besides, if no one comes to check the venue there's no reason for the upkeep you seem to admire." She replied.

"And admire it, I do. Can you show us around? We would love to see everything you have to offer," I said, trying to keep my excitement under control.

"Calm down, gumdrop!" Jake finally piped up, I almost forgot he had come with me.

"Jake Thomas Dawson, can I not be excited to marry the man of my dreams?"

"Um ...." he stood there speechless, shocked cause I only use his full name in times where he has done something crazy.

"I'll take that as a yes," I said, still full of excitement. "Now, Ms. Julie, please continue with helping us if that's alright." She didn't say anything, just turned around, and walked to the entrance of the Barn.

"Y'all have to follow me to see the inside," she laughed.

"Oh, right," Jake replied and we followed her into a rustic lobby area. "Oh wow, it's so pretty in here," I said all bright eyed, looking around at the rustic but classic atmosphere that the lobby provided.

"Yeah, Lady Belle ... sorry, Hannah. We have gone through three separate renovations of the space to make sure we can present couples with a venue that only compliments the beauty of their special day." She began to explain. "The newest version of our bridal and grooms' suites were built on the second floor on opposite sides of the hall. Both are always equipped with everything you may need on the day of the wedding. Would you like to see the chapel or the reception hall first?"

"Um, I don't know–Jake, what do you want to see first?" I said, turning around to see him off to the side, poking at some gold horses sitting on a nearby table.

"Jake!" I said firmly.

"Yes, gumdrop," He replied as his head shot up to look at me, which let me know he was paying attention to me.

"Do you want to see the chapel or reception hall?" I asked patiently.

"Um chapel, cause I can just ask what I want to know about the reception," He responded.

"Pastor Dawson, you don't seem to want to participate in the tour," Julie enquired.

"No, I do, just a little distracted" He replied.

"Oh, he helps me plan, it's just that he has socially checked out today. He has been updating friends back home." I responded in defense of him.

"Ms. Julie, I am also not as picky or detailed as Hannah is, so I'm easier to please. My only concern is how many it holds," he stated.

"Around a hundred seventy-two people can go in both halls" She laughed. "Now, if you can follow me around this little wall."

We walked around to a beautiful bucolic barn, perfect for our little country wedding. "We'll take it." I heard Jake quickly say.

I was sitting in my office preparing my first lesson for our women's Bible study group, while on the phone. Claire was sitting on the other side of the office, working on getting some stats on the church put together for me to look at.

"I hope I'm preparing the right message; I don't want to mess this up. They seem to be doing so well without me." I said nervously.

"You're going to do just fine. This is a part of the job; you must give them instruction. Remember what Romans 10 tells us," Bishop Travis, Jake and I's pastor said to me.

"Hold up, which part of the chapter?" I replied.

"Around verse 14," He said

I let out a heavy sigh. This man functions in his call as a teacher in the church 24/7, and will open scripture whenever he can. I turn to the scripture like I was told, reading the Apostle Paul's words with conviction.

14 How then shall they call on him in whom they have not believed? and how shall they believe in him of whom they have not heard? And how shall they hear without a preacher?

"Yes sir," I said, as a young teen girl with beautiful brown skin walked into my office. She wore black clothes with dark blues and purples. I adjust myself in my seat, "Hey Bishop, I have to go. I'll call you later when I've left the office."

"Hey, can I help you?" I asked.

"I was looking for Claire. She has something for me" she replied.

"Go behind the counter in the kitchen, all of yours and Kyle's stuff is there. Before you leave though, this is Pastor Hannah, one of the new lead pastors."

"Um, hi Pastor Hannah, I'm Sydney," She replied.

"Hi Sydney, how are you doing? Are you coming to the women's bible study tonight?" I asked her.

"Yes, ma'am," She responded and turned to Claire. "I will be ready around 5 o'clock. Does that work for you to pick me up? I have to go to the home first, and make sure Kyle takes his meds."

"Yes, I got you Sydney, you know that," Claire responded.

I watched as she left the room, and headed down the hall. "They live in a home. No one in the church is willing to take them in?" I said with worry in my voice.

"Yes, Kyle and Sydney live at a group home. Most of our members are either too young to take them financially or too old physically."

"Oh my Lord. How long have they been living in a home?"

"Since their family died in a fire 5 years ago. They were only in the 7th grade," She replied. You can hear the sadness in Clarie's voice, the pain behind her words. "You know, their father was actually the pastor right before the one before y'all. That's partly why Sydney may be struggling faith-wise, but she will be the most dependable person here." Claire said calmly.

I look over at Claire, "Well, I'm making those two my business while pastoring this church."

"You look so good sitting behind your desk, gumdrop." I look up to see Jake standing at the doorway. "Jake, I thought you left for the day." I asked with confusion.

"I'm on my way out now. I was wondering if you wanted to go out for pizza before you teach the ladies tonight," He replied with a smirk across his face.

"I actually just have to go over my teaching, which I technically can do in the car." I told him.

"Is that a yes, gumdrop? Cause you've removed your only reason to say no." He asked.

"Oh, can I still say no?" I said with a half-smile. Standing up from my desk, I walked over to him, lightly touching his arm, and looking him in the eyes. "Yes, I would love to..." I grabbed my jacket, and waved Claire goodbye "Claire, I will see you an hour prior to Bible study starting."

CHAPTER 5

Hannah

As Jake pulled into the church parking lot, I brushed crumbs off my dress. "Thanks dear, I hadn't eaten anything since breakfast this morning before we left."

"You didn't doordash anything, gumdrop? You have to eat, no matter how busy you are working," He replied. "Do I need to order you food when I order mine everyday?"

"No, I just forgot to order something," I replied.

"Ok, I'll be ordering you lunch from now on." He said firmly.

I looked at him and rolled my eyes at his stubbornness in making sure I eat, but I also loved it because it showed the sweet guy I fell for back in high school. "Whatever gives you peace, dear," I responded.

I get out of the car, and start making my way back into the church. All of a sudden, I heard a loud car horn. I turned around to Jake yelling, "That's my sexy future wife!"

I walk back up to his side of the car, "Jake Thomas Dawson, you can not do that on church property. I love you, but we're pastors. We must be an example for our members."

He looked straight at me "But was I lying? You're my future wife and you look very sexy. I think us being truthful is being an example to the members of our church."

I looked at Jake, trying not to laugh "That's not the point. Don't do that again, please."

"Okay, I'll stop, gumdrop," He said with disappointment.

I smiled and gave him a quick gentle kiss, then headed into the church. In the lobby, I am met with Sydney, Claire, and an older looking woman that if I remembered correctly, was Elder Crawford .

"Good evening, ladies," I said cheerfully.

"Welcome back Pastor Belle. I hope you enjoyed your bite to eat with Pastor Jake." Claire said. "Before we go in, I would like you to formally meet Elder Crawford. She has handled our women's ministry, since our last pastor stepped down."

"Sweetheart, I was in charge of the women's ministry while he was here too. His wife couldn't organize a stuffed animal's tea party if you told her to. Lord knows she was a piece of work."

"Well, it's nice to officially meet you. Let's not bad mouth the church's past leaders. Though, I bet they were great at leading the church to where it needs to be," I stated.

"Sure, whatever keeps you asleep at night," Elder Crawford smirked.

I shook my head as we entered the sanctuary to join what looked like around 40 women for Bible study. Claire pointed to a front seat, and told me to sit there.

I walked over to sit my Bible and binder with my notes, as Julie came to greet me. I smiled and quickly gave her a hug, "Mrs. Julie, how are you doing today? I was wondering if you were going to be here tonight."

"I'm doing wonderful, you are good to go with the venue for the wedding on July 23rd for your summer barn wedding," She said. "I can't wait to see how beautiful of a bride you'll make. I'm almost upset that I have to wait 3 months to do so." She chuckled.

"I'm so excited for it." I replied.

I take my seat after deciding to greet all the other ladies after Bible study. I looked up to the front of the church to see Claire and Elder Crawford getting ready to start Bible study.

"Alright, let's go ahead and get started. Right before we get Pastor Hannah up here, Elder Crawford will give a few important announcements you need to be aware of." Claire cheerfully said.

"Ladies of Redemption Fellowship, next month, we will be having our quarterly Women of Strength service. Our speaker will be Sharen Miller of Grace City Church out in Autumn Ridge, VA." She announced. I looked around at the many women, who were about to hear me teach. *Lord, help me feed your people, show me what each person needs to grow their relationship with you. These are your children, nothing here is mine.*

"And now, we would like to present to some and introduce to those who missed this past Sunday's service; Pastor Hannah Belle." Claire said.

I stand up and make my way onto the stage. Claire hands me the microphone. "Good evening, Redemption Fellowship women! I'm so glad to share the word of God with y'all. Tonight, I would like to teach from the topic 'A Poured Out Heart' from 1 Samuel chapter 1," I said with all the confidence I could gather.

CHAPTER 6

I stood in the middle of the dressing room, overcome with disbelief that I was getting married in a little over 2 months. I remember dreaming of my wedding day in middle school, me and my friends would plan every detail together. I'm pretty sure my mom still has my bright pink binder, that I put everything in. I met Jake a year after creating it. I heard a knock on the door breaking my train of thought.

"You can come in," I replied. I watched as the door opened. Two of my best friends, Savannah and Emma Grace walked in. They are twin sisters that lived across from me growing up. Our moms say we met at 2 years old, and we were inseparable ever since.

"Hannah, what is taking you so long? Are you sewing the dress?" Savannah Grace said.

"No, I'm not sewing it, though we both know I could. I was actually getting ready to come out." I responded.

"Yeah, cause Mama Shepherd is on her third glass of champagne," Emma Grace said.

"Oh Lord, let's go show my mom and sister this dress."

I followed them both down the hall to an open space where my mom, my sister Hope, and Sydney were waiting. I step onto the little platform facing everyone, "Oh wow, it's so beautiful," I heard Sydney say.

"You're a beautiful bride, my dear," my mother told me.

"Thank you so much, mom," I said, then I began to turn around to judge how I looked in the mirror that was behind me.

The dress was a beautiful mix of both the trumpet and mermaid silhouette styles. It had an off the shoulder neckline with beautiful lace.

"It's perfect! I think I've found my wedding dress. It has the elegance I wanted, the lace doesn't reveal anything, and it has the most beautiful appliques."

"Hannah Belle Shepherd, you look as sexy as ....." Emma Grace started to say, then looked over at my mother.

"As what? Emma Grace, please continue what you were going to say. Don't let me stop you," my mom said firmly, giving her a death stare every southern child grew up to fear.

"Ok, moving on to getting your dresses picked out." I said, trying to shift the conversation. I turned to the shop's worker, "Do y'all have any flutter sleeve dresses? Possibly in a light blue?"

"Yes, we do. All I would need is each bridesmaid's size." He said, pointing to one behind him.

"That's great! I will email you that information later," I responded.

I make my way to the register to pay for my wedding dress. "Let's go ladies. We need to go grab something to eat. I'm starving."

"Of course, let's get some food for this bride quickly. Jake will have our heads if we let her go hungry," Savannah Grace laughed.

As we walked out of the bridal shop, I saw Savannah Grace grab onto Sydney. "Hey Sydney, so tell me, any cute boys at that school of yours?" She asked.

I glared at Savannah, wondering what she was up to. There were so many questions to ask. Why this one? "No, I'm more focused on my studies," Sydney answered nervously.

"Oh come on, you don't have someone you wish would take you out?" Savannah Grace pried.

"Like a date? Oh god, no! I'd much rather read in a corner somewhere than go on a date," Sydney moved close to me.

"Sydney, what kind of books do you read?" Emma Grace asked, trying to rescue Sydney from her sister's invasive questioning.

"Fantasy stories and a few romances here and there," She answered.

"Okay ladies, we have arrived at Daisies Dinner Table. Our lovely lunch spot for today," I said as I led everyone into the diner.

As we walked in, Daisy met us with open arms, "Pastor Hannah, I am so glad you are here." she said.

"It's good to see you Daisy, did you get my text about reserving your private room?" I asked. She smiled at me, "Yes, I did get that text, and everything is already set up."

"Thank you so much Daisy," I replied.

I gave Daisy a tight hug, and started my way towards the rear of the restaurant. "Ladies, follow me to the back, and let me dazzle you with some good southern food fixed by Daisy and her kitchen staff."

"So Sydney, what kind of romances do you read?" Emma Grace asked as we walked into a small room with a long family style tale set up in its center.

"Um, it depends on how I'm feeling, I'm currently reading The Nazrite's Vow by Mavis Henson. It's a really cool Samson retelling," she answered.

I looked over and smiled at Emma Grace, trying to have a conversation with Sydney to make it less awkward for her. She has always done that, even in school she would find the most lonely or out of place classmate, and make them feel like they were the coolest person in the room.

"Hey Emma Grace, thank you for making Sydney feel like she's a part of the group" I said.

"Of course, Sydney seems like such a good kid, her parents must be so proud" Emma Grace responded. Sydney shifted around in her seat nervously "Um, my parents died in a fire a few years ago."

"Oh you poor thing, do you stay with family?" Mama Shepard.

"Sydney, I am so sorry! I didn't know" Emma Grace said with a regretful tone.

"It's fine, I promise. Also I don't live with my family, me and my brother live in a home." She replied.

I glare over at my mom to give her a warning not to push the matter, she looks at me giving me an unforgettable death stare. I sat up in my seat and picked up my phone to let Jake know that we were at Daisies getting food.

I looked up at Hope, "Hey sis, want to be my maid of honor" I asked.

"Um, I thought that was a given," she laughed. "Though, I do have to ask ... Can I bring Alexander to the wedding"

"I don't know who that is." I replied.

"He's my boyfriend," she answered back.

I almost spit out my tea, "When did you get a boyfriend?"

"Two weeks ago, he's in my church history class," Hope laughed.

I shake my head, and then checked my phone, I look up at everyone, "Looks like the guys will be joining us for lunch"

"Oh dear lord, hope they cleaned up first." Mama Shepherd said.

"Mom, they were just at a tux fitting," I laughed.

CHAPTER 7

Jake

I stood in front of the mirror looking at my black tux with a light blue necktie and vest. I almost couldn't believe I was marrying the woman of my dreams, my sweet gumdrop, Hannah Belle Shepherd. I remember back in high school, when she would cheer for our high school's football team. Since I was one of the team managers, we would go out for ice cream on the way home. Hannah loves ice cream, it was the one thing I could get her that brightened her smile after a bad day.

"Man, if dad could see you, he'd be so proud of you" Casey said, placing his hand on my shoulder.

I give him a faint smile. "Okay how does everyone's tux fit? Does anyone need adjustments to be made?" the tailor said, coming from down the hall.

"My tux is a bit loose," my other brother, Dallas, spoke up. I looked over at Dallas trying to adjust his tux jacket, so that it didn't look like it engulfed him.

"That's more than a little loose," Jace, my closest friend, said as he took a sip of his root beer. I laughed, "Oh lord, you may need to go down a size or two. How did you get the wrong size?"

"Man, I don't even know," Dallas responded and looked at the tailor. "Can I return for another fitting?"

"Yes Sir! If you come in later this week, I can measure you again, then fix the suit to fit. It will be adjusted and ready in time for the wedding." The tailor answered.

My phone goes off, I go to check it to find a text from Hannah,

> **We've finished at the bridal shop, and we are at Daisies Dinner Table for lunch**

"Okay. Does everyone else's tux fit correctly?" I asked. Casey and Jace both give me a head nod. "Okay good, the girls are over at some restaurant called Daisies Dinner Table. It's right up the street, and I'm thinking we should maybe crash their lunch."

"This won't go well, but what the heck. I can go for a bite to eat" Casey laughed.

"I guess we're crashing their lunch" I said, grabbing my root beer, and went to the dressing room to change out of my tux.

I thought about how Hannah would react if I showed up without a heads up. She wouldn't mind at all, though she doesn't like surprises. So while taking off my tux jacket and dress shirt, I sent her a text that we were coming.

> *We're just finishing up here, then we will join y'all there*

A text back quickly popped up on my phone screen ...

> *Oh, y'all want to join us for lunch? Cool*

> *Are we not allowed to join y'all?*

> *Yes, y'all can join us, just didn't realize y'all were going too.*

> *Ok, I'll see you in a few, gumdrop*

I sat my phone down, and pulled my shirt down. I sipped my root beer, and walked back into the lobby area to all the guys fully changed and ready to go.

"Alright, looks like everyone is ready to go" I said walking over to the tailor to hand him my card, so that the tuxedos were paid for.

"Yep," Casey and Dallas replied in unison.

"Ok, once I get my card back we can go. The ladies know we're coming cause I remembered how Hannah doesn't like surprises."

The tailor handed me back my card.

"Thank you Mr. Gaines," I told him. "Ok guys, the ladies are up the street. When you get into your car, make a left out of the parking lot and drive down about 6 or so miles."

"Okay, Jace and I will go in my car," Casey said.

"Sounds good, Dallas you can ride in my car" I responded.

We all walked out of Mr. Gaines' Tailor Emporium, and got into our respective cars. I put on my seatbelt, and took a glance over at Dallas in the passenger seat. "You may want to put on your seatbelt, you're in the car with The Homecoming Truck Race Champion."

I started up my truck, and hit hard on the gas, revving my engine. Casey rolled his window down and yelled "You sure you want to do this? I can wait till your bachelor party to leave you in the dust, Jake?"

"Bring it on, I'll beat you now and then" I responded back to him with full confidence.

"As you wish Mr. Preacher Man" Casey laughed while rolling his window up, and drove out of the parking lot.

"Oh, you unclaimed roadkill" I laughed following him out.

"Isn't this what got y'all in trouble when you were younger?" Dallas asked

"Yep, we do these three to four times a year for fun. It's also how I crashed Mr. Shepherd's truck" I reply. I love tapped the gas pedal, eating Casey and Jace to the next stoplight.

Casey pulled up next to us with his window rolled down "You burned dinner roll, guess we're playing dirty"

I didn't even glance over "I don't know what you mean, I'd never play dirty. Cleanliness is next to godliness you know" I responded then pulled off.

I heard my phone start ringing, I took a quick glance at my phone to see My gumdrop at the top with a few red hearts next to it.

So I hit a button on the steering wheel to answer it. "Hey gumdrop, I'm on the way now."

"Oh I know, I can hear you and Jace revving your engines at each other from here" she replied.

"Well, technically Casey is driving the other car" I laughed.

"Not the point, I bet this is why you wanted your truck down here" she responded.

I drove up in front of the restaurant, "Well, I'm outside now, so I'll see you once Casey pulls up" I replied. I looked over to the right of me, and three cars down was Jace and Casey, with Jace in the driver seat.

"Ok see you when you get in," she replied before hanging up.

I walk over to Jace and Casey "Hi guys, how long have y'all been here."

"Oh not long, though we did see you pull in thinking you won" Jace laughed.

"Y'all are some cheaters, I want a rematch" I responded.

"Oh you will get that rematch, I don't know if it will change anything though" Casey replied.

"Ok whatever. Let's go in, the ladies are waiting for us." I told them.

CHAPTER 8

Jake

I sat at my desk preparing to go to a church board meeting, "Finley, where is the paperwork on the ministry participation for the board meeting."

"It's in your email's inbox, you just have to send it to the printer." He answered.

"Thank you, do we have anything before the board meeting?" I asked.

"Nothing, though you did say something about calling Kyle." He responded.

"Yes, thank you for reminding me about that, I'm going to have you and Kyle help the children's ministry until we get a children's pastor" I said.

He looked at me disgustedly, "Please tell me you're joking, dude."

"Nope, I'm not joking" I replied.

"Hope you find one fast then." He said back.

I picked up my phone and dialed Kyle's number, after about two rings, Kyle answered. *"This is Kyle."*

"Hey Kyle, this is Pastor Jake, I'm calling to let you know that we need you and Finley to help the children's ministry, while we look for a children's pastor."

"Ok, no problem. I can help the children's ministry," he replied.

"Thank you Kyle," I say with relief. "Also, are you sleeping at the home or at my house tonight?" I asked

"I'm legit sitting in my room at your house right now" He laughed.

"Oh ok, I'll make sure we bring dinner. If you need any food before that, let me or Hannah know and we'll doordash you something," I told him.

"Yes sir," He replied.

I hung up the phone and started gathering my stuff. "Finley, can you get the paperwork from the printer please?"

"Already did, while you were on the phone." He handed me a small stack of paper of ministry participation stats and applications for children's and youth pastors.

"Ok thank you, let's head over to the conference room," I told him.

We walked out of my office and began to head down the hall. I stopped at Hannah's office door, and gave it a quick knock.

"Come in" I heard her say, I opened the office door to her sitting at her desk with Claire and Sydney sitting on the other side. Hannah looks up towards me, and smiles. "Is it time for the meeting already?" she asked.

"Not quite, you got about twenty minutes till then, me and Finley are just heading over earlier," I replied

"Oh ok, give me ten and we'll be right over," she said.

"Oh also, I'm ordering lunch for after, so think about what y'all want." I told her.

"I got a taste for some Mexican," Sydney replied.

"Same, though if we wait till tomorrow to get Mexican food, we can get it cheaper. They have 45% off every thursday." Claire said.

"Well we can't get Chinese, we had that twice this week already," Hannah said, looking as if she was in deep thought concerning lunch.

"Just let me know when you get in the conference room," I told them, annoyed at them overthinking food.

"Love you dear, see you in ten minutes," Hannah laughed.

"Love you gumdrop ... I mean Pastor Hannah." I replied.

I close the office door, and start down the hall once again. Finley looked toward me as if he was lost. "I forgot to tell you Bishop Travis texted me saying he was here and waiting in the conference room."

"Wait, Bishop is here! That's just perfect, he wasn't supposed to be here till Wednesday to help with the interviews for children and youth pastor candidates." I replied.

"Well, he is waiting in that room for all of us," Finley said, and pointed to the conference room door. Finley looked at me, as if he was waiting for me to tell him to cancel the board meeting.

"It's fine, Finley, you can go ahead and open the door. Bishop being here doesn't change anything, it just wasn't expected."

Finley opens the door to Bishop Travis, Elder Crawford , Deacon Wesson, and Elder Vines sitting around the table with three boxes of a dozen donuts.

"Good evening everyone, I hope you weren't waiting too long." I said, as I entered the room.

"Don't worry Pastor Dawson, we haven't been here long," Elder Vines said. "Speaking of which, hello Fin. I believe I raised you with manners or did you forget them out wherever you were last night?"

"Dad, this is not the time or place, it is my place of work, we can talk about this at home." he replied.

"*Mhm*, keep acting like your painted nails are the only sins you commit every week," he said with a roll of his eyes.

"Oh ok, I don't know what I just walked into, but Elder Vines you are out of line. Finley is correct, this is not the place or time for that. Whatever problem you have at your home, fix it at home." I turned around to find that it was Hannah addressing Elder Vines.

Though I'm very blunt in how I communicate, Hannah never wasted time in correcting people in their wrong.

"Lovely for you to join us, Elder Belle, now we can start this meeting, and get some actual work done." He replied.

I quickly looked over at him. "That's Pastor Belle, you will not discredit my wife just because she corrected you instead of cosigning with you, trying to address home issues, in a meeting that was scheduled for church business. We were hired to pastor this church, and that's exactly what we both will do."

"You mean your fiancé?" he smirked.

I looked over at Elder Crawford and Bishop Travis. "Elder Vines, no, I meant my wife. You are dismissed from this meeting. We are only discussing the applications for children and youth pastors today, your presence isn't required for that."

"Now to the rest of us, I'm sure you have met Bishop. He is a great man of God, he is the one who trained me for ministry. He is and will always be Hannah and I's pastor."

"Well, from talking to him while we waited for y'all he seems like a wonderful man of God. Pastor Dawson, may we start now?" Elder Crawford asked.

"Yes, Elder Crawford, start our board meeting please."

"Okay, no problem. We have a few people who applied for both positions from old fellowship churches, though many of them don't have the best of character. Oh, I almost forgot the opening prayer, Deacon Wesson can you pray for us please?"

"Will do Elder Crawford," He cleared his throat. *"Dear heavenly father, we come to you to ask for you to bless this meeting, gathered to help govern a local flock of your people. Guide us as we make decisions best for their development. Amen."*

"Amen. Thank you, Deacon Wesson." She smiled. "Now, as I was saying, we have many candidates with great experience, though their references didn't come back positive."

"So, we can't hire any of them. Do we put out a call for more? I sadly don't know y'alls process prior to me and Jake becoming lead pastors," Hannah asked.

"Pastor Belle, we would normally, but this was our third round of possible candidates. Now it's whatever we decide at this meeting or the next, but we have to make a decision soon."

"If I may, Jake, is Casey still in town? I can send him down here to be the youth pastor." Bishop replied, sitting up in his seat.

"Um, I believe he just left yesterday," I replied. "Did you ever train him for ministry? I know it was a conversation before we were sent out to work here."

"Oh, he was already in training. We just didn't know if we wanted to ordain him yet" He replied.

"I will talk to him about coming for an interview to be your youth pastor. Also, are there any members that operate in the pastoral gift, that is great with kids in-house." Bishop said, looking over at Elder Crawford.

"Well there is Asher and Elizabeth Bennett. They currently run the children ministry, and they have shown that they have the grace for leading it. They do fit all of our requirements, including that our current church bylaws state that our pastoral staff must be a saved, married individual, or couple."

"That sounds promising, we will vote when Elder Vines is here …"

"Dear, he is standing outside the door, he didn't leave," Hannah said.

"Oh, he doesn't need to be here to vote, he is only on the board because his great great grandfather built the church. We have tried removing him, but haven't been successful. Some of our former board members shared his thought patterns and methods." Elder Crawford said.

"We trust you Pastor Dawson, you have our full support," Deacon Wesson said.

"Okay, I will get Finley to reach out to the Bennetts, and Bishop, if you can speak with my brother Casey. Next meeting, we will sit with them both and make final decisions together. I will also ask Claire to get together with Elder Crawford to put together a report about Elder Vines' work here at Redemption Fellowship. Meeting Adjourned!"

CHAPTER 9

I pull out the pizza out of the oven, placing it on the island. "Jake! Kids! Pizza is ready!" I yelled out to my home of three.

Jake walked in, grabbed his plate and picked up three slices of cheese pizza. I gave him a slight glare, wondering why he needed three.

"Oh God, you're glaring at me like my mom. What did I do this time?" He asked.

"Nope, I'm just glad I cooked two pizzas tonight, cause Kyle and Sydney need to eat."

"I know they have to eat. Matter of fact, where are they?" He replied.

"In their rooms most likely, not knowing I called them down for dinner."

"I can go up stairs and grab them. Also Hannah, what do you think about possibly adopting Kyle and Sydney." Jake said, looking me in the eye. That's how I know when he is serious about something and it has hit his heart hard.

"Um, I would love to adopt them, though I question if it's financially responsible for us. Plus we are still navigating being pastors in a new town."

"Gumdrop, if we were to actually do it, God will remain faithful. Also finances aren't a problem, God's not just *Abba*, he's *Jireh*," He said while giving me a quick kiss.

Before he could pull away, I grabbed his shirt to keep him from stopping the kiss too early.

"Shepherd, you know there's no premarital making out, teasing me like that will get you in trouble," He laughed pulling away.

"Y'all know there are other people here right, or did you forget," Kyle said standing at the kitchen door.

"Yes, we know you're here Kyle. Get a plate and grab some pizza. Also, it's movie night so head to the living room after you finish."

"Ok, Pastor Hannah. Also, Sydney is on her way down, she said something about finishing a chapter of some book about Samson," He replied.

"I'm already behind you doofus," Sydney laughed.

"Ok you two, get your pizza and join us in the living room, we're watching *Play The Flute*."

I grab my plate and a glass of sweet tea, walk over to our living room and sit next to Jake as he pulls up the movie. I feel a slight pull, I look up at him and smile.

"Nice try, Mr. Dawson," I slid closer to him and took some of his blanket forcing him to share.

"Look, I did it just to get your attention, to finish our conversation on adopting the twins. Nothing more than that," he smiled.

"Ok sure, that was your reason. How about we pray about it, and mention it to Bishop Travis for his opinion."

"And also get the foster home's number, for when you say yes," He replied.

"Yes, we will also get the foster home's number"

"Why do y'all need the foster home's number? You are not going to try and adopt us, are you? Great, we're going to be preacher kids again." Kyle sighed.

"As your Pastors, we want to make sure you have everything at the foster home."

"What we need is a place to call home again," Sydney replied.

"No we don't, we are fine where we are," Kyle glared at his sister.

"Do you mean here at the parsonage or the foster home? I can only agree with one of those, Kyle," Sydney said.

"The foster home is better than being on the street," Kyle snapped.

"And an actual home with guardians is better than the foster home." Sydney snapped back.

"Are you that quick to move on and replace mom and dad, Sydney?" Kyle continued to snap at his sister.

"You realize our parents are dead right, Kyle? I hate to say it, but they are not coming back." Sydney said, yelling through tears.

"Ok guys, calm down, we just want to make sure you have everything you need. If that means working on getting someone to adopt you, then we can try and do that. Though, let's make something very clear: no one will ever replace your parents, and if they treat adopting that way, they don't need to adopt you."

"Ok, let's not look at *Play The Flute* tonight, I'll drive y'all back to the home, we can watch the movie another day." Jake said.

"Promise?" Sydney looked at Jake with tears still in her eyes.

"I promise, Sydney. You have my word," he replied.

"Sorry for all of this, we've been through a lot, and we sometimes don't have a safe place outside of each other to express how we're feeling, and it just leads to arguments like this one." Sydney told us while wiping her tears from her face.

"Sydney, never be sorry for having emotions, it's what you do with those emotions that matters."

"Sydney and Kyle, go get in the car, so I can take you home." Jake told me, "I'll be back after I get them home."

"Ok, be safe please? Also, can you bring some ice cream back?"

"No problem, gumdrop," Jake said, kissing me on the forehead.

"Thanks, dear" I smiled at my future husband. I got up after finishing my pizza to clean up the kitchen.

As I put the leftover pizza up, and the dirty dishes in the dishwasher, my phone rings.

"This is Hannah!"

"Hey Hannah, I need your help, but you have to promise you won't tell mom." Hope's voice comes through.

"Hope, that doesn't sound good, if you're asking for a Shepherd's Oath"

"It's Alexander," she replied.

"Is everything ok? He didn't touch you did he?"

"No, nothing like that. Alexander just told me ..." She tried to say through tears.

"Ok Hope, here's what we're going to do. Jake and I will be up there later this week. I will help you then. For now, just cry as much as you need to."

I hear the front door shut, Jake must be back from taking the twins home.

"Here is your ..." He looked at me, "Who do I need to fight now?" He said.

"No one, at least not yet. Hope called saying Alexander told her something, and it has her crying,"

"Who the heck is Alexander?" He asked in anger.

"Her boyfriend, dear."

"May I have the phone?" He asked. I nervously handed it to him, not knowing what he might say.

"Hey Hope, your brother-in-law here. We will be there by tomorrow evening," He said angrily and handed the phone back to me.

"Sir, we have work at the church to deal with that is time sensitive. We can go up later this week like we planned for the cake tasting and deal with it then."

"Nope, we will drive up in the morning. Now excuse me, I'm going to call Finley to make sure we get an elder to be a speaker at bible study, and the guys to get our guns" He replied walking up the stairs.

"Where's my ice cream?"

"In the bag" He answered.

"Dear lord, don't let this man do something crazy, or at least give me the strength to deal with the mess afterward. Amen"

CHAPTER 10

Jake

We drove into my mother's driveway after a long drive back to our hometown. "Oh lord, my back is killing me. I hope mom has some pain killers."

"If not, I'll get some for you," Hannah replied.

"What would I do without you, gumdrop?"

"You would still be in that house, and not a college graduate pastoring a church in a small town 4 hours away," Hannah laughed.

"That might be true."

"Only maybe," Hannah said with a smile.

I laughed as I got out and made my way to Hannah's side of the car to open her door.

"Oh Lord, y'all finally made it. I've been up for hours waiting for you to arrive." I hear from toward the house.

I look up, while opening Hannah's door, to my mother and groomsmen standing on the porch waiting for us.

"So, who's giving our guns some long awaited action?" Jace asked.

"Oh dear Jesus, is that why y'all were at my door at five in the morning? There will be nothing of the such," she said firmly. "Lord, y'all are too much like your father. Even you Jace, He loved you like the 5th son he never had," she said, fighting back tears.

Casey walked up beside her and gave her a gentle hug to comfort our mother. She looked over at him with her warm southern smile.

"Ok, enough with talking about your late father, boys. Come on in the house, I got a good Dawson Southern breakfast with Hannah's name on it."

"What about me, mom?" I asked.

I stood there lost for words, longing for the food that filled my childhood memories, now shared with someone other than my siblings.

"I fed you until y'all moved to Edmond. You'll be fine if one isn't for you," she answered.

"Don't worry dear, I'll share," Hannah laughed.

We walked up the stairs and gathered hugs from everyone.

I looked around, and Jace must have known who I was looking for. "Chloe is in the dining room with Audrey," he told me.

"Oh, okay, I was wondering why I didn't feel her grab me by the legs."

Jace followed me inside and we laughed at the thought of Jace's 3-year-old daughter attacking my legs like she does every time I visit Jace.

I walk into the kitchen, where all the memories of freshly baked cookies, cakes, and homemade hard candy every week after school. It was the bonus of having a mom who went to culinary school and had the town's favorite bakery and restaurant. *Before you ask in disbelief, yes my mom owned and managed both while taking care of 4 sons(some say 5) and a daughter.*

I walk into the kitchen to see Audrey fixing two plates of food. As I get ready to say hi, I feel a pair of little arms wrap around my legs.

I look down at Chloe, and pick her up in my arms "Hey buddy, helping grandma in the kitchen this morning?"

"More like she's getting in the way trying to either eat or play with everything in sight." Audrey replied while handing Jace his plate.

"The real question is how long do we have to wait for a little Jake or Hannah running around." Jace spoke up through a mouthful of pancakes.

"Very far from now, if I have anything to say about it, " Hannah responded.

"Well, don't make us wait too long, I still gotta get you back for all the stuff you spoiled Chloe with, when she turned 2 last year" Audrey laughed.

"Oh y'all hush, they will have kids when they are ready, though I'd love to see grandkids before I die" my mother smiled. "Now pray tell, what brought y'all down days early, you wasn't suppose to come up till Thursday"

"We're here to help my sister, Mama Dawson, you remember Hope right? Her boyfriend made her upset, so mental damage control has arrived" Hannah told her.

"Jake Thomas Dawson!"

I turned around from a pan of cheese and eggs, to my mother giving me a death glare with her hands on her hips. "I know darn well, you did not call your brothers to meet that boy with your guns in hand." she said firmly, and it was worse than if she would have yelled.

"We just want to scare him a little," I replied, scared myself looking at my mother as she spoke.

"Have you no shame, all of you go put your guns in your dad's old safe. You'll get them back when you leave for home" she said, looking at each of us.

"But mom, he hurt ..." I began.

"In the safe now, I need no response" she said, stopping me mid sentence.

We all leave the kitchen, and go down the stairs in the hallway to the basement or what we called it "The Dawson Men Lounge."

This is where our dad took us and many of our male friends he mentored. He would use the space to decompress, but also to teach us what true manhood was.

As we reached the bottom of the stairs we saw that the safe door was still open from the night we found him dead after defending his family from a robber.

After the funeral, we each took our guns. Well everyone but Charlie and Dallas, Charlie had passed years before this, and Dallas was a middle schooler then. Both of their guns are still kept in the safe.

We left Charlie's gun with mom, and prayed she knew how to use it. We've never seen her use one, and she refuses to go to a range with us.

"Hey remember when Dad first got us each a gun, he said we need to know how to use it to defend our future families properly." Casey laughed.

"Yeah, he was very clear that if we weren't defending family or hunting during hunting season to leave the gun in a safe." I added.

"That man taught me everything, He's the only reason I can be a proper husband to Audrey" Jace said as tears fell down his face.

"Okay pixies, let's get to the kitchen before mom comes after us down here," I told them.

"You're not helped, that was the most Dad thing you could say" Dallas laughed through tears.

CHAPTER 11

After we had a hearty breakfast at Mama Dawson's house, we got a few more hugs from everyone before heading over to my parents' house.

"Okay, before we go in, please do not make a big deal out of this. We don't have all the facts yet,"

"Don't worry, I won't do anything crazy, gumdrop. I promise," Jake replied.

"At least your mom called off your brothers and took your guns. You getting arrested two months before our wedding was something I really didn't need."

"Of course gumdrop, that wouldn't be good," He laughed.

We got out of the car and walked to my childhood home's door. Before either of us could knock, the door swung open to my mother standing there with a disappointed look on her face.

"I know darn well you were not going to knock on the door of a house you still got a key to," she said.

"Mom, we just wanted to be respectful, and not just walk in."

"Nonsense, now does your coming home days early then planned have something to do with the crying mess of your sister upstairs?" she asked.

"Yes, it does," I answered my mother with a smile.

"So are you going to tell me what's going on?" she asked firmly.

"I don't fully know what happened, and I'm under Shepherds Oath to not tell"

"Dear lord, why did your father teach y'all that mess? Well, come on in, Savannah and Emma Grace are up there with her now." my mother shooed me into the house.

I walked into the house and went straight up the stairs.

"Remember when we got caught making out in your room?" Jake laughed.

"Yep, it was your first ever Shepherd's Oath. My father joked that you had to sign the book with blood." I said, trying not to laugh.

"That wasn't funny. I was truly scared about that." Jake said.

I knock on my sister's bedroom door, waiting to hear her tell me to come in. Nothing ... weird, she always at least responds when someone knocks on her door.

I open the door to find her sitting on her bed with her hands covering up her face. Savannah and Emma Grace on either side of her in comfort.

I walk in and sit directly in front of her. "Hope, I'm here ... look at me, your sister is here to help you"

She looks up to see me smiling at her. She reaches out to me for a hug. I pull her to me and hold on to her before saying anything else to let her know that her big sister had her back. After a while, I lifted her head up and wiped her face.

"What is he doing here?" she asked, pointing to Jake.

"Hope, he came to take up for you. If it wasn't for Mama Dawson taking guns, him and his brothers would most likely be in jail by now"

"Guns!" Hope replied

"Don't worry, we were stopped, but just know we are ready to go at the drop of a dime. All we need is a text." Jake laughed.

"Wait, y'all took out the guns for this. I haven't seen y'all do that since Charlie—well nevermind." Emma Grace said.

"You can say it Emma Grace, I've done all my crying about it, and to not talk about him would be a disservice to who Charlie was." Jake replied.

"Now that, that's over with. Hope, what did Alex do?"

"He broke up with me, " Hope said, fighting tears.

"Do we know why he did it," Savannah Grace asked

"He said something about strengthening his relationship with God." she said

"Isn't that a good thing?" Jake spoke up. I gave him a quick glare. "This isn't something I can help with, I'm going to go get a glass of water" He said, realizing this maybe a girl to girl talk.

"You do that" I laughed

"Jake was fine, it was after I overheard his friends asking why he was dating a church girl." she answered.

"Oh lord, what did he say in response?" Emma Grace.

"He didn't say anything, just nodded at them. Yesterday evening he call and broke up with me" She cried

"Well, it sounds like it was for the best sis. Though it's not the end, I have hope that God will send you someone who will love God and love you." I said wiping her face again, "Remember Hope is your namesake," I smiled.

"Thank you Hannah. You always know what to say" she smiled back.

"Do you want to go explain all this mom, you got her worried."

"Um, you three are under Shepherd's Oath" she said firmly.

"You need to at least tell her y'all have broken up"

"I guess, can we all go and get donuts for Dawson's bakery?" she asked.

I smiled at my sister, she loved donuts from the Dawsons as much as I loved ice cream, it was the thing that always made her smile.

"I do you one better, if you talk to mom about this, I'll call my Mama Dawson personal to get us some sweets"

"You're lucky, married into the family that has the best food in all Autumn Ridge." Savannah Grace said.

"And you're lucky, cause I'm marrying Jake, and your sister dated Charlie."

"Oh the dates we would have at the bakery during his lunch break" Emma Grace said..

"Trust me, my wedding may be in Edmond, but there was no way I wasn't getting my cake and catering done by Mama Dawson." I laughed.

"Imagine if you'd grow up with her food everyday for school" I turn around to see Jake standing in the doorway with a glass of water in hand.

"We did, we were at her restaurant everyday after school." Savannah Grace laughed.

"Y'all legit gave me my lunch, which she sent everyday when I was in school." Emma Grace said.

"Oh Hope here is some water, you need to drink some after all that crying sis" Jake told her,

"Thanks Jake," Hope laughed. "Ok, y'all owe me some sweets, let's go"

We all walked down stairs to the kitchen, where my mother was cleaning.

"Oh y'all got her out of her room" mom smiled and hugged Hope. "will you finally tell me what's wrong"

"Alex broke up with me, but I'm fine now, " Hope answered.

"Well, I'm glad you're fine" mom said, and kissed Hope on the forehead.

CHAPTER 12

Jake

We sat in the parking lot of Dawson's Divine Sweets, my mother's bakery that sits next to her restaurant.

"Well, we better get in there, my mother has been waiting for this since we met in high school."

"Yeah, she asked me about cake flavors right before homecoming." she laughed

I got out of the car and made my way to her side to open her door. We interlocked our hands, and walked into the bakery to my mother behind the counter.

"Oh my, premarital hand holding, Jake Dawson you rebel ." She laughed.

"Mom, you're not funny."

"I thought she was funny," Hannah replied.

"Oh course you do, you have to kiss up to your mother-in-law before the wedding."

"She has to do no such thing, now get back here before I tell you you can't have cake." my mother said.

"That's not fair, I'm getting married."

"I don't think she cares," Hannah replies, and gives me a quick kiss on the cheek.

"You know a few more of those, may make me feel better."

"Just come on," Hannah laughs.

We finally walked toward the back, where my mother waited behind a table with 10 little cake squares, with her hand on her hip. "I didn't realize you had to take a bus to get from the dining area to the bakery's kitchen.

"Don't worry, I just had to give Jake a kiss to get him to move on from your threat of no cake." Hannah replied.

"That sounds like Jake" my mother joined in, with laughter. "Now, we have 5 flavors for you to try."

"They all look so good to me," I said

"You just like sweets Jake," my mother replied with a smile. "This first one is an almond cake layered with St. Germain strawberries and St. Germain Chantilly cream."

I pick up a fork and grab a little of the cake square, "Oh, that's really good, though I'm not a ig strawberry fan"

"I agree, this one is really good," Hannah smiled.

"The next flavor is a more mature funfetti. It's a vanilla cake with specks from some edible flowers, Vanilla cream cheese frosting" My mother explained.

Already tasting it, "I think, I want this one gumdrop" I said, still eating my cake square.

"Jake Dawson, I am not having funfetti, as my wedding cake" Hannah said glaring at me.

"Not taking up for Jake but I am doing six layers, so you can get more than one flavor, you just have to find another flavor that pairs well with it"

"Wait six layers, I thought we said three when we last talked"

"Was it, I thought you said six over the phone" my mother replied.

"Nope, I'm pretty sure I said I needed a 3 layer cake"

"Now, I think this red velvet with cream cheese based buttercream frosting would go great with the funfetti"

"Oh, that's really good." Hannah said "I like this one Mama Dawson"

"You don't want to taste the last two," she replied.

"Um, can you pack it up and we eat them down the road, I don't want to give Jake anymore sugar"

"Yeah, if he downs a whole square again, he's going to crash hard energywise" my mother laughed.

"Y'all realize I'm right here"

"Yes we do. Hannah, here are the last two squares plus some other sweets for Sydney and Kyle." my mom said.

"How do you know about Sydney and Kyle"

"I called the house phone, one day and Kyle answered" she answered. "So, when does the adoption process start"

"We have to make a few calls, that's our first step"

"Do they know y'all are trying to possibly adopt them" she asked.

"Nope, not yet. Though they may know that it's possible."

"Well just know, I think it would be nothing less than a God-given blessing. Now get out of my bakery and go get packed, you have a church to get back too," she responded.

We hugged my mother one more time, and walked out of the bakery.

After packing all of our bags into the car, we said our last goodbyes to Hannah's family and my brothers.

We now have been driving for about a little over an hour, and have another 45 minutes.

I looked over to a beautiful sleeping Hannah, she had her back of her seat down, and was curled up with a lanklet that we keep in the car.

The closer we get to our wedding, the more I can't believe that the cheerleader from high school was going to soon be my wife. I reach over and push a few strands of hair behind her ear.

She began to stir up a little, so I reached over and rubbed her back a little to let her know she can keep sleeping.

"How long do we have till we get home, dear." she asked

"We got about thirty minutes or so, and we'll be back at the house. We can take the next exit in Silverleaf to get you some food though,"

"Um, I can go for a bite, I haven't had anything since, we did the wedding tasting with your mother," she answered.

I moved over to the far right lane, and took the exit to Silverleaf, North Carolina.

"So what do you have a taste for, gumdrop? Pizza, burger, maye some fish."

"Um, pizza sounds good, plus there is a local pizza shop ten minutes from us," Hannah answered.

"Nice, what street is it on?"

"It's actually right there," Hannah pointed to a restaurant sitting off of a corner off main street.

"Good eye, gumdrop."

"Thanks dear, should we get food for the twins, Sydney did text me that they'd be eating at the house," she asked

"Yeah, we can grab them a pizza as well."

CHAPTER 13

Jake

I was sitting at my office, when Kyle and Finley walked in.

"Finley said you wanted to see me, Pastor Jake," he said.

"Yes, both of you please sit" I pointed toward the chairs on the other side of my desk.

"Um okay, is everything okay Pastor Jake," Finley asked.

"Everything is fine, don't worry Finley. "I just was wondering if y'all wanted to get coffee with your pastor."

"I guess ... but why do you want to take us out for coffee," Kyle asked.

"I need to talk with you both."

"Oh, What did we not do to you likely," Finley laughed.

"I shall ask again, waiting for the answer. Are y'all willing to get coffee with your pastor, who only wishes for a bit of conversation."

"Yes, we are willing to get coffee with you." Finley answered.

I finished the email I had been working on and grabbed my keys. "Okay, let's go."

We all got up from our seats, and walked out of the office. "Kyle, I know you are used to the passenger seat, but Finley needs to sit there, due to him being my assistant."

"That's fine," He replied.

As we get to the front lobby of the church, we see Sydney walking in, wearing a sky blue hoodie sporting the question "Can I bring my sword." with a blood stain and sword.

"Oh cool, they came ... wait Sydney, why are you wearing my hoodie, the dusty rose one was yours," Kyle said.

"Are you sure, I thought this one was mine." she said innocently.

"Nope, you got the wrong one again," he replied.

"Sorry Kyle, I'll make sure I return it tonight."

"It's fine, I'll be back, we're going out for coffee."

"Okay Kyle," she replied.

After waving Sydney goodbye, we were on our way to Saint's Den.

"Ok, now that we have our coffee and food. Let's get started," I said, as we sat down at a table near the front.

"If we must, let's get it over with," Finley responded.

"It's nothing bad, we're just having a simple chat."

"Oh a simple chat, so you're not going to lecture us at all. It doesn't seem very pastoral," Kyle smirked.

"Ok, I just wanted to sit y'all down over coffee, and thank y'all for leading the children's ministry while we look for a new children's pastor."

"Oh, it was no problem, we love working with the kids of Redemption," Finley replied.

"Yeah, I've enjoyed doing story time every Sunday with them," Kyle laughed.

"Have y'all found the new children's pastor yet." he then asked.

"I think we have, though don't worry. I'm going to need y'all to help the new pastors transition smoothly."

"You want us to help them transition." Finley laughed.

"When they first start, it's going to be rough with it being a new church for them. So I need y'all to help me."

"We can do that, right Fin," Kyle asked.

"Yep, we definitely can help the new children pastors when they get here." Finley answered.

"Good, y'all hungry! We can get some food while we are here. Kyle, can you go order me a ham and cheese croissant?" I handed him my card and turned over to Finley "What do you want, Fin?"

He looked up at me, with disbelief in his eyes. Then as I feel the regret of using his nickname that I didn't have permission to use, I see him smile.

"I'll have the same as Pastor Jake," He replied looking at Kyle.

Kyle looked back and forth at us, and walked away to go order our food.

"Hey Pastor Jake, thanks for taking up for me at the board meeting the other week." Fin said.

"You're welcome, though I was only setting order within the meeting. It wasn't the place for your father to bring up a home issue."

"Well still I appreciate you doing it," Fin replied.

"Now, understand that you still must understand how to allow scripture to guide your life. Elder Vines may have chosen the wrong time and place, but he is still your father, who you must honor."

"I know, it just seems hard to honor someone who barely can embrace me with love," Fin expressed.

"Listen, neither I nor your father will understand your choices or make them for you. Though, trust me we love you, and will help you grow in God the best way we can."

"Why are you so different then other pastors I met." Fin asked.

"Well, no matter if you know biblical truths or not, we are commanded to do everything in love. I strive to do that everyday, because I would hate to stand before God, and be questioned about damaging your soul. " I spot Kyle coming back. "Doing the same as others doesn't bring change, now does it?"

"I guess it doesn't," Fin laughed.

"Ok, three ham and cheese croissants, one for each of us," Kyle said, sitting down in a medium sized brown bag.

"Good, let's go, we'll eat it in my office."

"Wait, we're not eating here," Kyle asked.

"Nope, what made you assume that?" I laughed, and got up from the table, and headed outside. "Y'all coming or are you staying here?"

"You're our ride, we don't really have a choice," Fin laughed.

"Right you are," I said, while holding the door open, waiting for them.

"I'm too hungry for this," Kyle whined, while walking out of Saint's Den, which caused Fin and I to laugh.

CHAPTER 14

Jake

"Hey Jake, Can you get the door? Sydney just texted me that they're outside," Hannah asked.

"How did they get here, neither can drive."

"The social worker dropped them off, they are going to talk to us about the steps we need to take," she answered.

I look over at my wife, as she pulls out the last pizza out of the oven.

She looked back, "What, we have to be informed on what to do if we are truly doing this."

"I didn't say anything." He said, and went to open the door.

"Hey guys, come on in. Hannah just pulled the pizza from the oven."

"Sup Pastor Jake," Kyle responded. "Oh also, this is Mr. Bowdry, our social worker."

"Nice to meet you, Mr. Bowdry. I'm Jake Dawson, me and Hannah lead a local church called Redemption Fellowship."

"I'm aware who you are, Pastor Dawson," Mr Bowdry replied.

"Well, come on in. Hannah is in the kitchen."

I led them into the kitchen, where Hannah had cut the pizza, and was now pouring cups of sweet tea.

"Good evening, guys," Hannah said, while hugging Kyle and Sydney. "You can grab some pizza and a cup of sweet tea. Play The Flute is queued up on the TV."

"Hannah, this is Mr. Bowdry. The twins' social worker."

"Hi Mr Bowdry, I'm Jake's wife Hannah." she replied. "Would like a cup of sweet tea or maybe some water," she replied.

"No thank you Pastor Hannah, I'm just here cause you needed information possibly adopting the twins." he responded

"Yes, we haven't fully decided yet, but what are the steps we would need to take?" I asked.

" Well, the first step is for you to take the TIPP-MAPP course, it's technically optional, but I highly recommend you take it." He assured me.

"Okay, where do we go to take the TIPP-MAPP course? " Hannah smiled.

"Well normally you would do it through an agency, but I can get you in the course through the social service office. That is if you are going through with adopting them."

I looked over at Hannah, and how excited she seemed at the idea of us adopting Kyle and Sydney. "Yes, we are going through with adopting them."

"Great, after the course is a home study, then normally you would find a kid to adopt. Since you already have kids to adopt, we will meet about a transition plan." He replied.

"After that we make everything official through the courts. Right?"

"Yes, you are correct. It all ends in a judge making a final decree of the adoption." He said. "If there aren't any more questions, I'll let you enjoy movie night with the twins. I'll see you soon." He replied, leaving out of the door.

Hannah looks over at me with her sweet tea at hand "I didn't even have to move a muscle on this one. I serve a move making God." she laughed.

"Yes, we do. Let's go watch the movie with the twins, they've been watching without us for a while now."

We picked up our dinner, and headed into the living room to see the movie still paused.

"You realized that you could have started the movie without us right."

"We didn't feel it was right to watch it while y'all were talking to our social worker." Kyle replied.

"Aww listen, movie night isn't about the movie." Hannah smiled.

"It isn't," Sydney questioned.

"No, it's something me and Jake do to make sure we spend time together. That's what it's aout, cause how can you grow a relationship with a person you never see," she laughed.

"Darn, sexy and smart. My girlfriend may tell me I can't hang with you anymore."

"Guess, I'll have to sneak out the back." She replied.

"Nah, she would still see you. It best we just act as if nothing happen and pay off the children."

"Jake Dawson, you are silly, also I'm your fiancé. I left the title girlfriend when you put a ring on my finger." she replied, and kissed me.

"Was the dating pool small or– " Kyle joked.

"Nope, I just loved how kind hearted he can be, no matter how silly he is at times," Hannah replied.

"And I just saw a beautiful girl who was smart enough to deal with my crap, but also kind enough to give me a chance even after seeing it."

"Look, we have our challenges, and sometimes I want to fight Jake in the backyard. Though, I wouldn't trade him for anyone else to see at the altar next month." Hannah said.

"Okay enough with all this sappy stuff, let watch the movie."

"Can we please, couldn't agree more," Kyle said.

Sydney grabbed the tv remote and pressed play and we spent the rest of the night watching the movie like the family we would soon be. It was all I could ever dream, having a family of my own that truly loved each other.

Hannah looks over at me "you okay."

"Yeah, just thinking about how I always wanted a family like my mom and dad, and it may happen sooner than I thought."

"The heart of man plans his way, but the LORD establishes his steps." she replied.

"Is that Proverbs 21:30."

"Yes it is dear" she smiled.

I give her a gentle kiss and smile, for she truly is my helpmeet, and I'd have it no different.

CHAPTER 15

Hannah

Hannah and I were sitting in the conference room with Bishop Travis and the church's executive board waiting to interview our pastoral candidates.

"Well, if we all don't agree here, we'll just have lead pastors," Elder Vines said.

"Vines, this only a formality, and even if it wasn't, the church would be just fine with me and Jake as the only pastors. That's what equipping members for ministry is for."

"Correct, being a pastor isn't the only way God calls someone to ministry," Jake added.

"That's for sure, because I could never pastor a church, they are too attached to the leader." Elder Crawford said.

"Elder Crawford , the church requires many different gifts and callings to function. You are exactly where you need to be."

The door opens and Finley and Claire came into the room looking like they just got into a fight.

Claire fixes her hair and wipes her mouth "Casey has arrived, ready for his interview."

"Thank you Claire, you can send him in. Also tell Finley, that you two need to come in here as well."

"Yes, ma'am," Claire responded, and left the room.

"This is why I said we should hire people who are more mature to assist our pastors," Elder Vines complained.

"I disagree this allows them to serve within the church, and gives them the access needed for mentorship." Jake replied.

"You have an answer for everything, don't you Pastor Dawson?" he smirked.

"We were taught to carefully consider the effects of how to handle those we lead."

The door opened to Finley and Claire walking in and sitting next to Jake and I.

"Where is Casey, did you not go get him?"

"He was right behind us, I don't know why he didn't walk in." Finley replied.

"Sorry I'm a little late coming in, mom wanted to pray before I was interviewed, and who am I to stop her." Casey said, standing at the door of the conference room.

"Sounds like Momma Dawson," I laughed. "Okay if you can take a seat, and Jake will introduce everyone."

"Of course Pastor Shepherd," he responded.

I looked over at Jake, who was trying his best not to laugh. I gave him a quick glare to get back on track.

"Ok Casey, you know Hannah and I already, next to us our assistants Finley Vines and Claire Barnes. We also have board members: Elder Hunter Vines, Elder Frances Crawford, Deacon Kevin Wesson, and of course you know Bishop Travis James." Jake said, going through everyone.

"It is nice to meet each and everyone of you, and I am grateful for this opportunity," He responded after.

"Who has the first question for Casey,"

"Can you tell us about your training and education? " Elder Crawford asked.

"I have a bachelor's of biblical studies from Liberty University, currently in my master's program studying church history online. I was formally trained and mentored by Bishop Travis James." Casey replied.

"Will you have an issue juggling your master's and pastoring the Redemption Youth" Elder Crawford asked.

"Not at all, what I learn in my master's program, I plan to use to engage the kids in a question safe environment. I also hope that by doing both I will show the kids good time management," He replied.

"Casey, You said something that piqued my interest. You used the phrase 'question safe environment' can you unpack what you mean by that a little more?"

"Yes I can. It is my belief and option that when we train our children, it is important that we should encourage them to ask questions. How can they have a good strong relationship with a God they can't converse with, so I hope to foster an environment that allows them to do so." He responded.

"Don't you think that undermines both you and God's authority," Elder Vines piped up.

"Not if done correctly Elder Vines. You don't have to answer every question or inquiry of theirs. However, if we are to truly help them grow in God, some questions must be answered." He replied.

"Okay, I'm going to stop us right here. I believe we have heard everything we need. I will call you, after we discuss." Jake said.

"Okay, so how do we feel about the candidates?" Jake said.

"I love them all, they will be an excellent addition to our pastoral team," Elder Crawford replied.

"I will have to say I agree," Deacon Wesson smiled.

"I think the interviews went well, though I question if Casey will be up for the mental and emotional weight that is being a pastor," Elder Vines said

"Dad, what do you know about being a pastor, you've never been in the position," Finley snarked.

I looked over at Jake, wondering if he was going to correct Finley, or ignore based on the fact that Finley wasn't completely wrong. Elder Vines was never a pastor, so how would he know the mental or emotional weight of it?

"Ok Fin, you need to apologize to your father, his lack of experience in a position doesn't mean his concern doesn't have merit." Jake replied, correcting Finley

"No Pastor Jake, there's no need, I don't need an empty apology from my son. I know he doesn't respect me." Elder Vines.

"Ok I will meet with you both later, let's get back to our new hires," He replied.

"I assure you Pastor Jake, it will not be necessary," Elder Vines responded.

"Oh yes it is, I have an assistant who can't stop fussing with his father, who is an elder of the church. Scripture dictates to deal with your home, then God's. So we will meet later, or you can just stop functioning as an elder now."

"Yes, Is there anything that anyone thinks would stop our candidates from doing the job in excellence?"

I heard a collective no from everyone, and sat there marveled at how my soon to be husband took control of the room, seeing it kind of gave me a rush.

CHAPTER 16

Jake

I walked down the stairs to find Hannah humming, over a plate of eggs, turkey bacon, and french toast.

"Morning gumdrop, breakfast smells good," I said, after giving her a gentle kiss. I grabbed a piece of bacon off her plate.

"Jake Dawson, your plate is over on the stove. No need to steal my food," She answered.

"So I hear you're doing a new sermon series on Faith today." She laughed.

"Yeah, this awesome woman I know thought it was a topic worth taking some time on."

"Such a wise woman," she replied.

"I know, I heard she's marrying a local pastor."

"Well aren't I so lucky, I got private access to the pastor," she smiled. "Now go get dressed, Claire is driving us, and she'll be here in half an hour," she said.

"Yes, ma'am!" I finished up my breakfast, and walked back up the stairs to my room to pick out an outfit. I opened my closet door, and pulled out my Ultimate Redemption Unlocked Hoodie, white undershirt, and blue jeans. Now, I just have to pick out the perfect shoes to wear. I put on a simple pair of dark blue canvas shoes. After this, I ran back down stairs to wait for Claire.

When I got to the bottom, I was met with Hannah in a blue floral print dress, just as pretty as the day I met her.

"Jake, it's rude to stare," she joked. "If you're going to kiss me you got two minutes, Claire just turned onto our street."

"You don't have to tell me twice," I grabbed Hannah. As soon as her lips hit mine, I was transported back to the night I proposed at Silverleaf University's Student Center right before college graduation. She stood just as beautiful, as she has always been.

I felt a tuck of my hoodie, pulling me back to reality.

"Jack dear, Claire is waiting outside to take us to the church." she said.

Hannah grabbed her purse, and we walked out of the house.

"Morning pastors, are you ready to go," Claire asked.

"Morning Claire, yes we are ready."

We walked over to the car, and I opened the passenger seat, and helped Hannah in.

CHAPTER 17

Hannah

I lifted my hand from Jake's shoulder, after praying for him right before he went before the congregation.

Jake gave me a quick kiss, and walked up on the stage taking the mic from Evangelist Williams.

"Praise God Redemption Family, as always I am excited to be before you this morning. Hannah and myself have had such a wonderful time getting to know you as a local congregation." He smiled over at me.

"This Sunday we will be starting a sermon series titled The Unseen Things. In this series, with the help of our elders, I will take through different passages of scripture, where our biblical ancestors' faith was shown strong and in many cases, it was strengthened." Jake began.

I watched Jake do the very thing he told my father he would be doing the next morning of homecoming night, when he crashed my father's truck.

"YOU DID WHAT!" My father yelled. So scared of what he would do to Jake, I spoke up "He was having some fun with his brothers and they– "

"No, He will not hide behind you, I'll deal with your current dating choices later." He interrupted me, saying.

"Dad, Jake is not like that!" I cried.

"I didn't ask what he was like, go to your room." He said

I looked over at my mom, expecting her to defend me, she just nodded her head at me, so that I would listen to my dad, and go to my room. So I turned around to go up the stairs, but I heard Jake clear his throat. I stop mid -stair, so that i could hear what he was going to say

"Sir, if I may say I am deeply sorry for crashing your truck, that you were so gracious to allow me to use tonight. I and some of the guys just got a little overzealous with it being our last homecoming. You know what that's like don't you, I know you must have some crazy stories." He said.

"You know what I do have crazy stories from my senior year, though I wasn't crashing someone else's truck in some Homecoming Race." He answered.

"No, You crashed your own truck James. At least this young man won," my mom laughed.

"You raced your truck on Homecoming too." Jake asked.

"Son, we're in the south, of course I did. Look the point isn't you racing, it's you being irresponsible with my truck. If I can't trust you with my truck, how can I trust you with daughter."

I almost lost my breath at this question, cause me and Jake never talked about anything beyond dating, when it comes to our relationship. I waited to hear his answer, I too was curious.

"Well she doesn't realize this, but I purposely applied to Silverleaf University, so we can get our degrees together. My plan is to marry your daughter after we graduate there, and I hope to pastor a church shortly after."

"Oh my, the truck crasher wants to lead God's people. Let your first lesson be stewardship son," my dad replied

I ran to my room and screamed into my room, never did I know I would date someone who also wanted to go into ministry, and I didn't even tell him I wanted to. It's strictly God's doing.

As I return to reality, I realize that Jake has preached most of his sermon and was closing out the service.

I looked around to make sure, no one saw me in my state of daydream instead of listening to the sermon. Though, I did hear it, as he was preparing, soo if I'm asked about any of it, it'll be fine.

CHAPTER 18

Jake

"**I**'m back from my walk, gumdrop," I said, as I walked in a house full of visiting family from both sides. There sat Hannah, Mama Shepherd, Mr. Shepherd, my mother, Hope, and several other brothers and sisters.

"There you are Jake, thought you were hiding from us for a minute." Casey laughed.

"No, I've started doing morning runs, that's all. Besides, you're moving here, so hiding isn't really a smart option."

"True, I'm just looking at possible apartments to send over to the board," He sighed.

"I thought you were going to build a house, you don't have to limit yourself to an apartment that RF offered you." Hannah replied.

"I know, though it's just me, and building is going to take some time," He said.

"Hopefully, that will change soon," my mother said.

"Mom, he doesn't need to marry before he's ready."

"That is true, though Jesus sent the disciples out two by two. A good wife will help him stay on the straight and narrow." Mr Shepherd spoked up.

"Ok, I would love to talk more about my brother's love life, but I'm hungry."

"Finley is bringing you 2 chicken biscuits and a coffee, from Daisies." Hannah replied.

"And that's more reason for me to marry you," I said, giving her a deep passionate kiss.

"Dear, our family is here," Hannah smiled, pulling away from me.

"Yeah, we don't need to see y'all practice your marital acts." Jace laughed

"It's nothing like that, we sleep in separate rooms to prevent any sure thing." Hannah laughed.

"I got breakfast for a pre-wedding family gathering," Finley yelled walking in.

"I told you to get Jake food, not the whole family. Our mother most likely will be cooking later," Hannah replied.

"She found out your family was here, down the grape vine. I got there and she just started handing me bags of food," He replied.

"Sounds like her," Jake laughed. "Take everything to the kitchen and everyone who wants some, can get some."

"No problem, I'll still hand you your chicken biscuits as well," He replied.

"You have a nice assistant, I'm surprised how young he is though," Casey said.

"Yeah, he is very hardworking. I didn't pick my assistant though, he was hired when we got here."

"Oh ok, that's good to know," He replied.

Finley walks back and hands me my food. "Thank you Finley."

"Hey Casey, do you remember Allison from high school? She's moved back and it looks like she is single," my mother said, circling back to wanting Casey to marry before he starts at Redemption.

"I do remember my ex-girlfriend, mom. I also remember why we broke up, don't you." he smiled, knowing our mother wasn't going to give up.

"Didn't she have a kid last year." Hannah asked

"Yeah, it's with the guy she dated after me. He went to the military, and she found he cheated after he left for deployment. She only came back to handle her late mother's estate." Casey replied.

"Wait, when did her mother pass?" Hannah asked.

"Last month, Allison is still there though, to make sure everything gets settled," He answered.

"I'm just saying, she still could be your helpmeet." She sighed.

"Mother, the woman is grieving!" Casey said.

"Well, think how great it would be if she had a good man, who would let her cry on his shoulder." my mother replied.

We looked at our mother and just shook our heads at her train of thought on Casey's ex.

"Jace, did Chloe got some ice cream."

"Yep, she dropped out in the grass five minutes ago." He laughed.

I look over his shoulder, at Chloe standing over her dropped ice cream that she had just gotten.

I turn over to the teens, sitting at the picnic bench, "Hey Kyle, take Chloe back over to Nicole's Ice Cream Parlor and get her a new cone please."

"You got it, Jake," He said and ran over to grab Chloe.

"Do you really trust him to take my daughter to get ice cream?" Jace asked.

"Yep, I've seen how he looks after his sister, Sydney."

"Ok, If you trust him," He said

"You have no reason to worry, I promise," I laughed

"What's y'all relationship with him anyway," Jace asked.

"Hopefully, they're still thinking about adopting him and his sister." my mother said.

"Mama Dawson, we haven't made that info public yet," Hannah replied.

"Leave it to mom to tell everyone something, that was supposed to remain private." Casey laughed.

"She's fine," I said. "Mom, we are in the process now. We are taking the encouraged course now, and our home study will follow after."

"Oh my, that is so exciting," Aubrey replied.

"Yeah, we can't wait to officially provide them a good home. Hannah came home crying, when Claire told her about their situation."

I wrapped my arm around Hannah, and gave her a gentle kiss on the forehead. She looked up at me with the most beautiful smile I have ever seen. Oh how I would do anything to keep her by my side.

"The way y'all look at each other, is so romcom, it makes me sick." Casey laughed.

"All I know is I am forever in love with Ms. Hannah Belle Shepherd, and can wait to make her Mrs. Jake Dawson."

"Yeah, even if I wanted to, I can't get rid of you Jake." Hannah laughed.

"That's because my brother is a parasite." Dallas joked.

"Dallas, I will snitch on you so hard, don't you even start."

"You have nothing on me," Dallas replied.

"Two words, Last Christmas."

"You wouldn't, and you can't," Dallas said

"Yeah Jake, Remember D10," Casey spoke up.

"What is D10, am I missing something?" Aubrey asked.

"You're married to one of these fools, and don't know about the Dawson Brotherhood Treaty. It is why they were all gun ready on our last visit." Hannah replied.

"Never heard of it," she responded.

"It's a two or three page document, unless you get it in booklet form, that lists out a bunch of stuff of five of them agreed to. For example, D3 is why Casey was Jace's best man." my mother explained.

"If a Dawson brother of the current generation finds a spouse, the prior brother shall serve as their best man."

"Ok, so y'all have a literal bro code," she laughed.

"Yeah, pass down from our dad. D10 just says that if we do something crazy, we can't mention it outside of the group."

"Y'all are the weirdest southern family," Aubrey replied.

"Yep, and you married into it," Hannah laughed.

CHAPTER 19

"Are you done getting ready? I was hoping to get to dinner by seven gumdrop." Jake says as he enters my bathroom.

"I'm almost ready, just getting the last of my makeup done, just give me ten minutes."

"So, wait to start the car in about twenty minutes," he laughed.

"Jake Dawson, I literally have to only pick out lipstick for the night." I pick up a bright red and a nude. "Which one do you like,"

"Ooo, I like a good nude lip, though you haven't done a red lip in awhile." He said.

"So again I ask, which one do you like?" I shook my head at his lack of answer.

"Let's go with red, it's date night of course," he winked.

I quickly put it on, grabbed some toilet paper and removed excess lipstick off. I turned around and looked over at Jake with a smile.

"Ok, you big baby. I'm ready to go."

"You know you love me." He smiled.

"Yeah, that's true unfortunately," I gave him a quick kiss. "Now let's go, you wanted to get there by seven."

"Well, look at my smokin' hot future wife. How on earth did I get so lucky?" He asked.

"An Angel came to me in a dream, said you need desperate help."

We walked into a local bistro that Jake googled. He said we needed a night of relaxation, due to all the work we have been doing at the church.

"Welcome to Edmond's Bistro. I'm Amanda, how can I serve you today." the hostess said.

"Hi Amanda, if we can get a tale for two please."

"Yes ma'am, right this way," she said, leading us to a booth just a few feet from the entrance we came through.

We sat down with our menus, and thanked the hostess.

"This is a really nice restaurant."

"You sound surprised that I found it." Jake responded.

"No dear, just stating that it's nice."

A small framed young man walked up to us "hi I'm Trevor, your waiter, you must be Pastor Jake and Hannah." he said

"We are indeed, how did you– do you go to the church?"

"Um no, I'm personally not religious. I'm a friend of Fin, he told me that he suggested this place to Pastor Jake. He told me to make sure I treat y'all well."

"I bet he did, he believes in good service," Jake laughed.

"That he does, and I don't like disappointing my greatest friend. Now, can I start you with some drinks?" He replied.

"Um, two sweet teas please."

"Coming right up, I'll return with," He walked off from the table.

I glared across the table at Jake "So you didn't find this place."

"I like to think of it as using my resources," He laughed.

"Not funny, you made me think you picked the place."

"Ok to be fair, Finley gave me a few choices, and because I knew his boyfriend worked here I chose it." He said.

Just as he said that Trevor walked up with our teas. I could see a bit of worry in his eyes, waiting for a figurative hammer to drop.

"Here are your sweet teas. Are you ready to order your food?" Trevor smiled.

"Yes, Can we both have a burger and fries. Also If Jake can get a milkshake after dinner, that would be great."

"Yes ma'am, coming right up," He replied.

"Thanks you Trevor."

He walked away from the booth, to give our order to the kitchen.

I looked up to see Jake just staring at me, the wonder I could see in his eyes was my favorite thing to watch.

"You know, the closer we get to our wedding, the more I feel more lucky to be marrying you." He said.

I reached over our table, and put his hand in mine. "I also feel really lucky that we are getting married."

He pulled me closer to him, and kissed me "Well, good we only have less than a month."

"Ok, quick change of topic."

"Sure gumdrop," He smiled

"How do you feel about the home visit with Mr. Bowdry."

"I think it went well, we just have to wait to hear back." He replied.

"Yeah, like that is truly easy dear, we are getting ready to get married in a few weeks. While also getting kids to take care of right out the gate."

"Most outside of our family think we are out of our mind," He laughed

"Good thing, they aren't our driving force."

As I said this, Trevor returned with our burgers and fries

"Here are your burgers and fries. Will you like for me to top off your tea?" He said with a smile.

"Yes please."

"No problem, I'll be right back," He replied.

"I can't wait to see you in your wedding dress, you're going to be the most beautiful bride." Jake said

"I just hope you and your brothers got the right suits."

"Do you not trust us to get work done? I'm offended gumdrop." Jake replied.

"I don't trust yall together at all, individually maybe."

"Ok that's fair, we are pretty wild." Jake laughed.

At that moment, Trevor walked up, and refilled our glasses with more tea.

"Let me know if you need anything else. I will bring Pastor Jake's milkshake in a few minutes as well." He said.

I gave Trevor a head nod, and returned to Jake who had already started to eat his burger.

"You must have been really hungry, did you even pray over the food?"

"Yeah!" He said, with a half eaten fry in his hand.

"Ok I believe you. Though please wipe your face, you have crumbs all over your mouth."

Jake grabbed the napkin that had been wrapped around his silverware prior.

"Sorry, it was a busy day trying to logically plan the staff trip to Bishop Travis's church. I had to skip lunch because of it." He replied.

"Jake Dawson, You gave me so much crap about making sure I eat lunch and you skipped lunch." I said, finishing off my burger.

"It wasn't purposeful, we were just that busy and focused on work." He laughed.

"I don't want to hear you fussing at me aout eating at the church again."

Trevor walked by and slid a styrofoam cup, and checked on the table.

"Thank you Trevor, don't leave just yet."

Jake grabbed his wallet out of his back pocket, and paid for our meal.

"Here is your tip, You served us with great excellence," I said, while handing him a twenty dollar bill. "And I hope you will visit the church one sunday with Finley. We would love to have you."

"Thank you Pastor Hannah, maybe I will," Trevor smiled.

CHAPTER 20

Jake

I stood in the church lobby waiting for Casey, who was teaching tonight. This was our way of slowly introducing him to the congregation.

"Excuse me sir, I'm looking for Pastor Jake Dawson. I'm the speaker for tonight." I turned around to find my brother, with the biggest smile plastered on his face.

"Haha Casey, Welcome to Redemption Fellowship Church, your soon to be church family."

"Were y'all this scared your first time?" he asked, as we walked into the sanctuary.

"Yes lucky for me though, Hannah preached on our first sunday. I didn't preach till two weeks later."

"Yeah, I don't have the privilege of a wife in ministry," He laughed

"I don't know about her being in ministry, but if mom has anything to do with it you'll be married by the end of the year."

"She has even started trying to pawn me off to one of her cashiers at the bakery," He said.

"'Did getting back with the high school ex not work out?"

"I haven't talked to Allison, mom thinks if there are options, I'd marry quickier," He replied.

"Sounds like mom," I laughed leaving him into the sanctuary of the church. "Let me introduce you to Evangelist Williams," I said, as I saw him walking our way.

"Pastor Jake, Deacon Wesson want to know if your brother needs a traditional podium or the circle table." He asked.

"Well it's good that he's right here. Evangelist Williams, here is my oldest brother and tonight's speaker Minister Casey Dawson"

"Oh, It is nice to meet you sir," He replied.

"I'm okay with whatever y'all normally use," He laughed.

"Well, Pastor Jake uses the table, but Pastor Hannah uses the traditional podium."

"Then, I'll take the table, Deacon Wesson doesn't need to be trying to carry that heavy podium."

"Deacon Wesson can out lift most of the men here," I laughed.

"Isn't he in his 60s?" Casey asked.

"Deacon Wesson is in his 70s, but he goes to the gym regularly. He also is always working on something, can't sit down, even though he is technically retired." Evangelist Williams replied.

"Correct, Evangelist Williams go let him know Casey's choice."

Right before it was time to go and introduce my brother as tonight's speaker. I turned over to Finley "Go grab Casey a bottle of water please, for while he teaches."

"No problem Pastor Jake," He replied.

The worship team started singing Reckless Love By Brandon Lake, which was the last song on the night's setlist.

"You ready, you're up in five?"

"I'm more scared then when dad took us to a gun range." He laughed.

"You'll be totally fine," The worship team was nearly done with the song.

"Sure, it's not like this is a job or something," He said, as he shifted back and forth.

"I got to go introduce you to everyone."

I made my way onto the stage, and grabbed a microphone from one of the worship leaders.

"Good evening Redemption Fellowship, If you don't know who I am, I'm Pastor Jake Dawson, and I will like to welcome you to our men's night." I smiled, looking into the congregation.

"We have a very special speaker tonight, my brother, Minister Casey Dawson. Who will be joining our pastoral team in the near future. I ask that you open your heart as he brings tonight's word from God." I handed the microphone to Casey.

I walked off the stage and returned to my seat, ready to listen to my brother preach.

Finley walked over "Casey has his water now, am I sitting with you like normally."

"Yes you're sitting on the other side of me" I pointed to the seats behind me."

"Ok good, Also I will like to formally introduce my boyfriend Trevor," Finley said as they sat down.

I smiled at the two of them, glad Finley was comfortable with bringing him to church tonight.

"Hi again Trevor, I hope you are enjoying our men's night."

"I actually am, everyone seems more welcoming than last time I was here," He replied

"I'm glad Trevor, you are always welcome at Redemption. I need you to know that."

"Thanks Pastor Jake," He smiled.

"I'll also have to tell Hannah, she missed you tonight."

"Yeah, make sure you tell her I said hi," He laughed.

"I most definitely will tell her, you said hi."

I focused back on my brother just in time to hear the last bit of his sermon.

"And just like Joshua, we must all make the decision that our homes will be God-centered. So I ask you what had to be asked of the Israelites, Who is on the Lord's side." He said.

I smiled at how great my brother looked preaching the gospel on the stage. I remember, when I told him I was going into ministry, he laughed at the idea of either of us preaching the gospel in the pulpit.

Evangelist Williams went back up on stage to do give the salvation call "Wasn't that word a blessing, Redemption give God praise for that amazing sermon on being on the Lord's side for Minister Casey Dawson."

I put my hand on my brother's shoulder as he returned to the front row "Good job little bro."

"Now you know you're wrong for that." He laughed.

I embraced my brother, and began praying over his spirit, one think I have learned for such is the need for prayer partners in ministry.

CHAPTER 21

Jake

"**M**orning Pastor Jake, you needed to see me before we leave for Victory Camp." Elder Vines said.

"Yes, sit down next Fin please," I said, pointing to an empty chair in front of my desk. "I need to discuss with you about your dynamic as father & son. If there are problems at home, it needs to be dealt with at home. At no point ..."

"Can I ask you something Pastor Dawson?" Elder Vines interrupted me.

"Yes sir, ask away Elder," I replied.

"Do you have kids at all?" He asked.

"Elder Vines, you are aware that I don't have children. It doesn't take away from the fact that in several meetings, you have taken cheap shots on your son. Which is very inappropriate to do, especially in board meetings discussing church business."

"Are you aware of what he does with the money he makes here? It doesn't all go in the offering plate." He smirked.

"Good, cause I'm not here for the check I'm given. What he does with his money is between him and God."

"Have you met Trevor, his lover? You have a gay man for an assistant," Elder Vines replied.

"Yes, He served me and Hannah dinner not too long ago. Matter of fact, He was at our last men's night." I laughed.

"Love that you think this is funny, Pastor Dawson," He replied.

"Elder Vines You must understand that no matter what sins Fin has, it is our job to train him in the ways of God."

"Pastor Jake, he's not going to hop off his high horse," Finley spoke up.

"Ok, here's what is going to happen. After Victory Camp, You both will be sat down from serving, Scripture tells us that you take care of the home before serving in God' house."

"Wait, how am I going to work? This is my job Pastor Jake," Finley protested.

"Don't worry, I'm going to cover the lost pay, and Kyle will take over till you return. You both have things at home that need tending to, so I as your pastor are requiring y'all to take a break."

"This job is the only thing that gives me comfort, please Pastor Jake," He cried.

"Oh son,you do have a heart," Elder Vines smirked.

I gave him a death stare, and made my way over to Finley. I pulled him into a lovely embrace, to let him know I was still here for him.

"Understand that yes Finley must honor you as his father, but his sin doesn't give you license to try to expose his struggles. It's actually your job to cover him."

I look at a upset Finley "You still welcome here, you and your father just needs to work on some stuff."

I heard a knock on the door, I looked up to see who was at the door.

"Hey dear, we're loading up the bus," Hannah said. "Is everything okay?"

"Yes, I'm just finish dealing with what we talked about last night."

"Got it! Do you need a few more minutes." she asked

"No need, we're ready to go," I said, as I got up. "Finley sit with me on the us please."

"Okay" she replied.

As the bus drove into Autumn Ridge, I looked over at Finley. "I talked to Kyle, and you can stay in his hotel room for the trip."

"Thank you Pastor Jake, seriously never as a pastor taken up for me." He replied.

"Oh course, I don't support sin, but I do support souls and their spiritual development."

"Most care so much of my lifestyle, that they negate how unloving my home really feels," He said.

"Finley, as long as I'm your pastor, I will make sure you are able to go through the process of salvation at your own pace. I only warn you not to make Jesus wait too long," I smiled.

The bus pulled into the Variant Hotel, and Hannah got up to give the staff next steps. I grabbed my bookbag that sat at my feet. "I'll be back, we have to go get everyone's room keys"

"Yes sir," he replied.

I got up and followed Hannah off of the bus. "How was the ride for you, gumdrop,"

"It was okay, I took a nap," she smiled. "Is Finley okay after the meeting? I saw he was crying."

"Yeah, he just expressed some stuff as we were driving in. I asked Kyle to let him stay in his hotel room, so that it gives him and his father time to process the meeting."

"I love it when you walk in your calling with confidence," she said, giving me a quick kiss.

We walked up the front counter to Allison. "Welcome to Variant Hotel! Oh Jake Dawson and Hannah Belle Shepherd, I haven't seen y'all since I graduated high school."

"Yeah, it's been a minute." I replied. "We are checking in, it's under Redemption Fellowship Staff,"

"Yes, just let me pull it up in the system." she smiled. "Here we go, if you can give me a minute to see if all the keys are ready."

We gave her a quick head nod, and watched as she went into a backroom off to the side of the counter.

"Do you remember Bishop doing the very first Victory Camp?"

"Yep, it's when he decided to ordain us as Ministers, almost 4 years ago." Hannah smiled.

"Oh the memories of younger us working during Victory Camp, not realizing that we would be bringing our church to it just a few short years later."

Allison walked out of the backroom with two big stacks of hotel room keys "Ok, here is all of your room keys. Names are labeled on the room keys envelope."

"Thanks so much Allison, it was nice to see you," Hannah said.

We went back outside to the us, and handed everyone their room keys.

CHAPTER 22

We all stood in one of Victory Christian Center's classrooms that are used for discipleship training.

"I am so glad that y'all was able to join us for Victory Camp," Bishop Travis said, as he walked in.

"Bishop Travis, great message as always. Truly you are a man of wisdom."

He looked over at me and Jake with the biggest smile. "I remember when these two met at our old shut-in, your man of God ran to my office in the morning demanding for all the information I had on her. After the first date, the only other thing I've seen him hold tight was a plate of food and Jesus."

"She started feeding me, she couldn't get rid of me even if she tried." Jake said.

"Good thing, I'm not getting rid of you." I said, pointing to her engagement ring.

"Alright you two," Bishop Travis laughed. "Out of all of the people I have trained, Redemption has gotten some of most unique ministers from my sons."

"You sure? I'm an idiot," Jake said, making all the staff laugh.

"You aren't an idiot, you just needed a good strong woman to keep you on track," Bishop Travis replied.

"Trust me, I got him."

"I know you do Hannah. Now, scripture tells us that God gives us pastors after his heart. I truly believe he has given you these two. Who's ordained among the staff." He said.

"Um, we only have a few. Elder Vines, Evangelist Williams, Elder Crawford, and Deacon Wesson." I replied. "Of course we have the Bennetts that are starting training, and Casey is in the process of moving to Edmond."

"We will look at the possibility of training others next year," Jake said.

"Sounds good!" Bishop Travis replied. "As the year passes, you will begin to get different resources from *Victory Christian Network*, stuff like your login to our membership platform, self paced college-level classes, yearly conference schedule, etc."

"Classes, are you questioning, if we know scripture," Elder Vines asked.

"Elder Vines, it's not that you don't know scripture. It's to give ministers the ability to continue learning, I even taught a few classes up there." Jake replied.

"Yes, I loved the class he taught called Relational Communication: A Study on Songs of Solomon."

"Behave yourself Hannah," Jake laughed.

"And we are always adding to the classes, so don't be surprised if you're asked about teaching one"

"Exactly Hannah," Bishop replied. "Jake and Hannah follow me back to my office, I will see the rest of you at tomorrow's morning session."

We gave our staff a quick nod, and followed him out of the classroom.

"Y'all are doing so well for only being there for a few months," Bishop said.

"That's good to hear, and Jake had to do a really hard thing before we left Edmond."

"The bisexual assistant or the accusing elder." Bishop asked

"Both, the elder is the assistant's father," Jake replied

"Ah, I forgot about that," Bishop laughed. "You sat them both down, didn't you."

"Yep, it starts right after this trip." Jake replied.

We walked up to the door of his office, and Bishop stopped in front of it. "Well, be glad you have a youth pastor coming soon." He opens the door to Casey sitting behind Bishop's desk.

It was a tradition of Bishop that when he sent out a new pastor they sat at his desk from which they were sent.

"Hi I'm Pastor Elect Casey Dawson, how may I help you." Casey laughed.

"Yes pastor, I need help telling my older brother I'm his new boss." Jake joked.

"Well, maybe instead of telling him that, you should model the Christian characteristic of humility for him," Casey replied.

"Okay you two, Casey come over here so that I can hug you."

"Yes, ma'am," Casey laughed. "Glad the team was able to come to Victory Camp this year."

"Yeah, we worked overtime trying to get together for it," Jake replied.

"And, I am truly grateful," Bishop said.

"Casey, you looked real comfortable in the bishop's chair. You know you're leaving here right," Jake joked.

"Thomas, shut up," He replied.

"Wow, middle name me. Did I offend you brother?" Jake laughed.

"Bishop Travis, can I send them two back here please."

"Boys, please don't make Hannah feel like she has to watch you like children." He replied.

"I think it's to late, she marrying Jake." Casey laughed"

"Ok, that's wild," Jake said.

"Look, Jake is the love of my life, no matter how childish he is with y'all."

"Hey!" Jake replied with his hands up in the air.

"Hannah, you're going to upset the child," Casey laughed.

"That's enough, the reason y'all are here is to discuss the vision of Redemption Fellowship as a church and how Casey and the Bennetts work within that vision as the other pastors there," Bishop instructed.

"The Bennetts didn't come to Victory Camp," Casey said.

"We'll have to video them after Bishop leaves, that's why we're here. The conference room's monitor is currently broken."

"Exactly Hannah," He said.

CHAPTER 23

I sat there as Jake packed for his bachelor party with his groomsmen.

"Do you have everything you need?"

"Yep, I don't need much," Jake replied. He walked into the living room wearing a white He Redeemed Me hoodie & a pair of tan khakis.

"Looking good dear," I grabbed a hold of him and gave him a kiss.

"Hey beautiful, can I get a few more of those from you?" He smiled.

"Just one more, you have to go soon."

"They can definitely wait a few minutes, they'll be fine," Jake said.

I give him another kiss, and feel him grab on to my hips tightly making it impossible for me to pull away. I lose my balance, and we fall onto the couch in a romantic bliss. I feel his hand move up to the side of my upper stomach.

I hear a knock on our front door, "Jake, your brother is here."

He quickly got up, rushing himself off, and went to open the door.

"Hello lovebirds," Dallas yelled as he walked in. "Oh, did we interrupt something."

"No, come on in Dallas," Jake laughed.

"Hannah, give you the marching orders for tonight yet," Dallas said.

"No, but you're about to get them," Hannah replied with a smile.

"Okay, let me go get the rest of the party," Dallas said, and walk back out of the house.

"Gumdrop, you can't be serious," Jake said.

"Oh I'm very serious, you and your brothers are mischievous."

Dallas walked back in with Casey and Jace.

"Okay boys, I can't stop you from doing something stupid. Including the fact that you most likely are going to race the two trucks sitting in my driveway."

"Hannah, you know us well," Jace laughed.

"I do! Which is why, if you hurt my husband before our wedding. I'll make sure y'all are injured twice as bad."

"Well that sounds like a challenge. You know we love a good challenge." Dallas said.

"Okay did you not learn your lesson, when she almost killed us after our fittings for racing." Jake laughed.

"When does a Dawson man ever learn their lesson? also you said husband, you haven't married him yet." Dallas replied.

"Okay Dallas Xavier Dawson, outside now!" Jace yelled

"Good lord, who do you think I am, Chloe?" Dallas snapped back.

"Dallas, outside or I'll beat you up like we're still kids in the den." Casey responded.

"Fine," Dallas said, walking back out of the house.

"Now that I have sent him outside, Hannah we will make sure that we are careful," Casey promised.

"I appreciate that very much Casey."

"Oh Elosie and James are arriving tonight as well, so she will be here in time for your bachelorette party," Jake said.

"Oh great, are they bringing Iris and Zoe with them."

"I believe they are, though they was discussing leaving them with some of James family."

"Ah, well I hope I get to see them."

"Gumdrop, you know how Elosie feels about her kids traveling too much." Jake repealed.

"But Auntie Hannah is family, family is a exception"

"Sure you are, though we never know what goes through Eloise's mind," Jake said, giving me one last kiss.

As the guys was getting ready to leave, Dallas runs back in.

"Didn't we send you outside?" Casey said.

"'You did, though I had to show these too in," He replied.

"You out there alone, we're all in here," Jake said.

"Just cause I moved a few states away doesn't mean I don't exist," our sister said, as she walked in.

"ELOISE!"

"Hey Hannah, did you miss me?" Eloise laughed.

"Um yes, of course," Hannah replied

"I thought y'all wasn't getting in til later tonight," Jace asked.

"Are you complaining?" Eloise replied.

"Not at all Eloise," Jace said

"Mr. Clement here sent y'all the wrong time," she explained. "Dallas go get your nieces please."

"So you did bring them," Hannah said.

"Why wouldn't I bring them? Was it a kid-free wedding," Eloise asked.

"No the boys had me thinking you weren't, due to not wanting them traveling too much," Hannah replied.

"Y'all are family, they need to see yall." She said, hitting each of her brothers upside the head.

"Ouch, we got a party this weekend, don't hurt us before we leave," Casey said.

"If I hurt you now, I have to worry about an injured brother at the altar or taking an injured boyfriend home," Eloise replied.

I felt an impact against my legs as two sets of arms grab onto them. I bend down to Iris and Zoe, with a big smile.

"Hey girls, it's good to see you. You grown so much, how old are you now."

They both quickly hold up three fingers, Eloise laughed "Zoe, you not the same age as your sister you're two years old little lady."

"They are so close in age that they're learning together, sometimes that means Zoe will copy what Iris does," James said.

"So cute," Hannah replied and gave them both a hug.

"Ok guys, we have to go over to the airbnb," Casey said.

"Yeah, we have to make a few stops first, so let go," Jake replied.

"Ok, I will see each of yall when you return," Hannah said. "We'll be here."

CHAPTER 24

Jake

We walked out of a grocery store with everything we needed for grilling at the airbnb.

"Lord, we have enough food to survive a week," James laughed.

Casey stopped mid-step "Why didn't you tell us Mr Shepherd was coming?"

"Um, cause I didn't think it mattered. He's going to be my father-in-law, besides who do you think was going to grill all this meat?"

Casey threw the bags that were in his hands into his truck. Then he gave me a look similar to how our father used to look at deer during hunting season.

"Ok guys, no need to fight with each other so close to Jake's wedding," Jace replied.

"Do you not remember the last time he interacted with the rest of us?" Casey said.

"Yeah, the weekend y'all all visited me a few weeks ago."

"He didn't even talk to us, what do you mean?" Casey replied.

"Well, it's to late cause they are waiting for us at the airbnb,"

"Well, you know what that means right," Jace smiled.

"Truck Race time," Dallas yelled.

"Okay, Dallas you come with me like always. James, you can go with Jace and Casey. Let's Race!"

"Wait, shouldn't James decide which truck he is joining." Casey said.

"Are you saying you don't want him, that's so mean of you."

"Guys, I don't actually care who I go with, we're going to the same place," James replied.

"We're going to the same place, but it's a race so they're still going to fuss over this," Dallas said.

"No, we aren't, I just thought we should be considerate of his choice," Casey said.

"You sound like you're running for office over at city hall. Whatever, he doesn't care what team he is on."

We packed up the rest of our bags into the trucks, and hopped in. I pulled out of the grocery store parking lot, and revved my engine at Casey.

He pulled up next to me at the red light, and smiled revving his engine back at me.

"Oh lord, here we go again," Dallas said.

"Oh yes, it's a must, Dawson men pass time," I said, as I hit on the gas, propelling the truck ahead.

Dallas looked over at me "You realize it took a left right, He's not even following you."

"Well that was stupid cause the house is right up this street, I know the person who owns the property."

"Okay Jake, but do me a favor, get your foot off the gas pedal," Dallas replied.

"Fine, you party pooper," I took my foot off the gas pedal. "We are almost there anyway."

"Wait what," Dallas said.

I laughed, as we pulled into the driveway. I looked to see Finley, Elder Vines, Kyle, and Mr Shepherd on the porch.

I get out of the car "Hey guys, Kyle I thought you was getting Finley."

"Elder Vines insisted that he bring him something about an opportunity to grow," Kyle replied.

"Well I wanted to make sure he was with a trusted adult. You're here now Pastor, so I'll see y'all sunday," Elder Vines said, while getting in his car to leave.

"Bye Dad," Finley yelled. "He lectured me the whole way here, then started asking your father-in-law his thought on my life choices."

"Oh lord, Mr Shepherd, how did you respond?"

"I told him I was going to mind my business," Mr Shepherd laughed.

I turned around to Casey pulling into the driveway next to me. He hopped out of his truck, running up to Dallas. "Dallas Xavier Dawson, you purposely texted me the wrong address."

"I did not, you just can't read apparently," Dallas laughed.

"Yall still race trucks, didn't you learn your lesson during homecoming years ago," Mr Shepherd said.

"Nope, we have not," Jace laughed.

Mr Shepherd shakes his head "Well, don't just stand there, get all the bags out the trucks. You still want me to grill, don't you?"

"Yes sir," I answered.

CHAPTER 25

Jake

"If you don't get away from this grill Dallas, you're going to meet my favorite rifle," Mr Shepherd said.

I heard this as I walked into the airbnb's backyard, and knew I should retrieve him. "Dallas, go get a root beer and leave him alone." I said, placing my hand on his shoulder...

"Thank you Jake," He smiled.

"No problem, Dallas can be a bit much."

"A bit much? He asked me if I was sure my wife really likes me." He replied.

"Oh lord, I'll talk to him, but he should be distracted for a while. Casey and Jace turned the living room into our own fight club."

"Y'all are children," Mr Shepherd laughed.

"No, we are just super close with each other."

He looked at me, as if I had told him that I was secretly a conman. "So close that my truck landed in a ditch homecoming night. So close that instead of getting summer jobs, you and your brothers spend your time pranking each other at your girlfriends expense. So close that y'all somehow missed the pain–"

I looked him straight in his face with disgust "Do you even finish that sentence? You know nothing of Charlie's death. Now if you'll excuse me, I'm going to return to enjoying my bachelor party with my brothers."

I turned around and make my way back into the house, walking in mid wrestle between Casey and Jace.

"Y'all realize that we can't break anything in here right, this isn't my property," I say as they bump into an end table.

James looked over at me "they would have been at it for over 10 minutes now."

"Of course, they have been, it's our normal."

James walked over to my side of the room, and handed me a root beer.

"Thank you man."

"Can I ask you something?" He asked.

"Yeah, what do you need man."

"How did you know you found your good thing in Hannah, or rather your wife?" He asked.

"You thinking of marrying my sister James."

He shifted a little side to side "Maybe."

I looked at him doing this and couldn't help but smile at the fact that I remember the night I decided I was going to marry her so clearly.

It was during junior year, I had a midterm the next morning and had planned to put an all-nighter studying for it.

Around 10:00 at night, Hannah called me to see if I had eaten dinner:

"What do you mean you haven't eaten yet Jake Thomas Dawson, Give me 20 minutes!" she said.

"You need to sleep, don't worry about me."

"Didn't ask for permission," she said, hanging up.

I laughed knowing she would be at my apartment in 10 minutes instead of 20. I opened my textbook back up to return to reading about The Protestant & English Reformations.

It was one of my favorite classes, I loved learning about church history and its effects of present day doctrine

I heard a knock on the front door, I got up and opened it for Hannah.

"You didn't have your key."

"Oh I did, I wanted to make you get up from your desk. Now, chicken nuggets or a chicken sandwich." She asked, holding both up.

"Nuggets of course," I smiled, grabbing it from her.

"Ok, you can eat the chicken sandwich later, I'll bring you some coffee in a minute," she said.

"You need to sleep, don't stay here trying to help me"

"I sleep on the couch, it's fine," she answered.

"I knew she was my wife, when I saw her as more than a romantic partner, but as a life partner who would encourage and assist me in being the best person that God called me to be."

Jace walked into the room with a hamburger in his hand. "Um guys, food from the grill is done."

"Ok, I'm going to go grab some BBQ, before the rest of you eat it all." Dallas said.

"No you don't," Casey tackled him.

"Casey, let him go please."

"Fine, but this isn't over," He replied.

CHAPTER 26

All the ladies sat around the floor of my living room eating pizza, after a long day of shopping and spa treatment.

"Ok, who's ready to watch a movie?" Emma Grace said.

"Shouldn't Hannah open presents first," Savannah Grace replied.

I looked at my friends, already aware what each of them had gotten me.

"I know the gifts already, and I'm very appreciative. Emma Grace gifted me a special edition set of Jane Austin—" I start to say.

"To keep romance alive," She finished.

"Savannah Grace's gift isn't here, which is worrisome," I continued.

"I promise it isn't that bad," She replied back.

"Hope brought me a beautiful teal tiara from high school, for my something blue."

I looked around at everyone and smiled "Should I stop, or do y'all to watch the movie like we planned."

"No, I can take it over from here," my mother said as she got up with a small box.

I reached out my hands, taking the box that I already knew it was my grandmother's earrings and necklace from her wedding to our grandfather.

"You're grandmother always wanted her wedding jewelry to be worn by generations of Shepherd women for their something borrowed," my mother said, holding the side of my face.

"Oh how I've waited to get these, since I was in middle school."

I smiled at my mother, not believing that in just a few days I was getting married to my high school sweetheart.

"Ok, we need to watch this movie before it gets too late. We have a busy few day ahead, let's get sleep while we can."

I heard the door open, I got up to see my soon to be husband walking into the house.

"Jake, she's supposed to be mine for the night, what are you doing here?" Hope said.

"Um, I needed something out of my closet," he replied.

"Sure you did, hurry up and get what you need," she said.

"I'll be quick, I promise" Jake said while running up the stairs.

"Jake just can't stay away, good lord," Emma Grace laughed.

"Listen, I love me some Hannah. Can you blame me?" He said, coming down the stairs with his bow and arrow.

I look over at him with a concerning glare "Now what on earth do you need that for?"

"He's going to do something stupid with his brothers," Hope said.

"No I'm not, just a game of squirrel hunt in the church parking lot," He smiled. "Gumdrop, you told us to keep busy, you never gave requirements to how to do that"

"Well be careful, I need you at full strength in a few days."

"Don't worry, gumdrop, I'll be safe," he said, giving me a gentle kiss on the forehead before leaving.

"Now, we can finally start our movie," Hope said, grabbing the remote.

CHAPTER 27

Hannah

"Oh my Jesus, you're such a beautiful bride," my mother said walking in with Mama Dawson.

I turn around to them both, with a slight smile, trying not to panic at the fact that it was my wedding day.

"Are you alright Hannah, you seem unwell," Mama Dawson asked.

"I'm fine, just a little nervous, now that the day is finally here." I replied, shifting side to side in my wedding dress.

My mom grabbed the sides of my face, forcing me to look her in the eyes. "Everything is going to be fine Hannah. You and Jake have already started to build a great God honoring life together."

I smiled at my mother and embraced her, knowing that she always knows just what to say. "Thank you mom."

We heard a knock on the door "Come in Julie;" I answered.

She came into the room "Hey ladies, how's it going in here."

"We just finished getting dressed, we just have to put on our jewelry," Hope answered.

"Savannah Grace is actually still getting dressed," Emma Grace said.

"Well that's fine, I am actually coming to get Hannah for the first look," She said

"Ok, Emma Grace please make sure your sister is dress before its time for the ceremony."

"Will do, Hannah," she answered back.

"I'll see yall ladies later," I said, as I followed Julie out of the room.

"Hannah, I asked Jake where he wanted to do the first look," Julie said

"Oh no, this can't be good," I replied, as we walked out of the barn.

"It sounded sweet, there's a giant tree on the property. He said it looked like the tree where he asked you out for the first time."

"Oh that is sweet," I said, as we walked up to the tree.

"Here you go, he's already on the other side, reach your hand around the tree with your back to it," she instructed.

I followed her instructions and backed up into the tree and reached my right hand around its truck.

"So gumdrop, you haven't run off leaving me at the altar yet," He laughed and grabbed my hand.

"And I never plan to you goof, you're not getting rid of me that easy," I replied.

"Good answer, Mrs Dawson," He said, pulling on my arm, causing me to spin around into his arms.

"Watch my dress, you will not ruin it."

"Oh, of course I wouldn't dare. Though may I take time to admire God's beautiful creation that stands before me. I may have to repent before the ceremony," he replied.

I hit him on the chest, as he looked me up and down. "Behave yourself sir, we still have to say I do" I said, giving him a gentle kiss on the cheek.

"Oh, just a cheek kiss," He said.

"Meet me at the altar, and maybe you can get one on the lips."

"Ok, everyone it's time to line up."

"Where's Jake, we can't line up without him," Dallas replied.

"He's walking in with Bishop Travis, out of the side door of the chapel."

"Did you not pay attention during the rehearsal," Casey replied.

"He wasn't paying attention at all, also where is his tie?" Eloise said.

"Dallas Xavier Dawson, go get your tie now! I swear if you boys mess up my wedding ceremony due to foolishness, it will take Jesus himself to keep me from committing murder."

"Ok Hannah, take a breath. Casey, go get your brother's necktie," Mrs. Dawson said.

"Mom, I can get my own necktie," he replied.

"You can get it, but I'm sending Casey so it's done in a timely fashion," she smiled. "Ok, while he does that everyone get into your places."

We all get into the line up that we was given during the wedding rehearsal "Dallas you're walking in with Emma Grace."

Casey walks back in, with Dallas necktie in hand. "Here you go Dallas," he hands it to him.

Behind Casey walks in Bishop Travis "Is everyone ready."

"Most are ready, Dallas just has to put on his necktie"

"Ah, well I'll tell Finley hit play on the speakers," He said, leaving out of the lobby.

I walk to the back of the lineup, and slip my arm into my dad's arm. He looks over at me with the biggest smile I've ever seen on his face. "You're such a beautiful bride, and will be an even greater wife," He said.

"Thank you dad," I replied, wiping away tears. "I'm going to ruin my makeup."

We hear the speaker cut on, but I don't know the song.

"Is that Skillet?" Casey laughed.

The music quickly switches to Everlasting Ground by Austin Brown. "Ok, now yall can start going in."

The wedding party starts slowly walking into the chapel. I looked up at the ceiling, as I became more nervous than I was before.

My mother looked at me "You want to pray dear."

I nodded at her, willing to help her daughter one last time.

She grabbed dad's and mine hand "Dear lord, help us as we step into this new season, you have called us to. Guide Hannah as she begins to start her own family, and helps her soon-to-be husband lead a house that will always worship you. Amen."

I looked up and Hope & Casey had just walked out. The music switched again, this time to Love Can Be by Rebbeca Rea.

My dad grabs my arm "You ready sweetheart?"

"Yes sir, I am," I smiled.

We began walking into the beautiful chapel, I looked at both sides with all of the smiles looking back at me. Then I looked up at Jake who was crying at the front of the chapel.

I smiled at him, and my heart filled with gratitude for a life partner I know I can count on.

We reached the altar, and my dad gave me a quick kiss and took his seat.

"Welcome everyone, we are here to witness the sacred union of Jake Dawson & Hannah Belle Shepherd. We come together to celebrate these children of God's decision that stand before us and thank all the family and friends who have joined us," Bishop Travis said. "Who gives this bride today."

"I do," My dad replied with a smile.

I looked at Jake and winked, He smiled at me. All of the memories of our relationship and how far we have come to get to this moment.

"Jake, Do you take Hannah as your lawfully wedded wife? Do you promise to support her completely and love her unconditionally, so long as you may live?" Bishop Travis asked.

"With every breath," Jake replied.

Bishop Travis turns to me, and asks me the same.

"I do," I replied, smiling at Jake.

"We will now exchange the rings, Jake, if you will," Bishop Travis says.

Casey hands him the ring, and Jake puts the ring on my finger. "I, Jake, give you, Hannah, this ring as a symbol of my love, commitment, and the eternal vows. With this ring, I thee wed."

Hope hands me Jake's ring, and puts it on his finger "I, Hannah, give you, Jake, this ring as a symbol of my love, commitment, and the eternal vows. With this ring, I thee wed."

"By power vested in me, by the state of North Carolina and Our lord and savior Jesus Chirst I pronounce Jake and Hannah as Husband and Wife, lawfully wedded before God. Jake you may now kiss the bride."

Jake grabs my waist pulling me into a passionate kiss, I grab ahold of the sides of his face, kissing him back.

"Ladies and gentlemen, it is with great honor that I officially present to you Mr. and Mrs. Jake Dawson!!"

We pull away from each other, and begin walking back down the aisle.

ACKNOWLEDGEMENTS

Wow, you don't know how grateful I am that you have made it to the end of this installment of a long journey of stories. You're so amazing, and I hope you enjoyed it.

This would have never been possible with so many people.

First, my mother and my grandmother who has supported me throughout this process. My father whose last name, my pen name bares.

Second, I would like to thank all my middle and high school teachers who encouraged me to write books.

Third, I would like to thank the online bookish community, who champion new authors and stories everyday.

Last but not least, the TPG Team in and out of house: Amanda Dalton. Abigail Louise, Juliet Thomas, C.A. Lovheart, Joshua Blanton Jr., and so many more.

ABOUT THE AUTHOR

Ty Williams is a Bible Teacher & Christian Romance/Thriller Author, who resides in Southern Virginia. He takes pride in writing relatable stories that bring honor to God and change humanity one book at a time. When he isn't writing, he's reading stories written by fellow authors, or researching some topic within history, mythology, or theology.